THE SHORT
SKIRT
FROM
INDIA

THE SHORT SKIRT FROM INDIA

Ruby Malshe

PARTRIDGE
A Penguin Random House Company

To order additional copies of this book, contact
Partridge India
000 800 10062 62
orders.india@partridgepublishing.com

www.partridgepublishing.com/india

CONTENTS

How can I forget ....

Yes, how can I forget to thank these few people whose patient ears and encouraging words helped me to write.

Michelle, Sandra, Harsha, Shalaka, Neeta, Loretta, Kshama, Milind, Arun and Michal, your little push was indeed a big helping hand to me.

In Praise of:

All the stories are deeply touching, profound, capable of disturbing sensitive souls and classy......

Prof. Arun Patil

For my daughters, who in their silence and noise encouraged me to write; writing being a source of delight to me.

STORIES FROM INDIA

Is life different in India? Do the people living in her cities of joys and sorrows and who wear the badge of Indian Citizenship have a heart, a mind and emotions different from the people elsewhere?

The stories in this collection showcase the oneness of mankind. Man-made boundaries may have different situational moments and perhaps even different reactions to those situations, but the emotions in each situation remain the same for every heart. A heart living out of India will cry when in pain, just as a heart living in India, will laugh aloud in moments of joy.

Though strife, death, pain and joys are universal emotions, they have a flavour of boundaries made by man dividing the world into parts, where each part has its own unique troubles and solutions.

For those who wonder about the kind of life the common people in India live, these stories lift the curtain of curiosity to let the world get a glimpse into the reality of my people covered in the cloak of fiction. Each story in a way is not imagined but real; for after all, fiction can only be produced in the background of reality.

The story of Poornima in 'Fear', involves choices and moral dilemmas of a war-torn heart not able to live without fear in spite of many years of peaceful living. In 'Contract', Shusmita has a shift in her perspective of life when the tenant at her flat in Mumbai, urges her to extend the contract in spite of the strict conditions laid down initially by her; but then faces her husband's death in spite of her pleas for his life with The Almighty. Parinita in 'I Need to Talk', silences herself forever when her husband Rajendra turns deaf ears to her requests to get a hearing about the tortures she is going through due to his mother's behaviour. Pervin, a young Zoroastrian girl in 'A Place in Mumbai', comes to the city for further studies and finds accommodation with an old couple who welcome her, in their longing for youthful company which gives them a silent assurance of help in their old age. Kishori, a little girl's story, throws light on the sorry state of life of our young children whose parents have enrolled themselves in the rat race of some superfluous achievement and fail to see the effects of the same on young minds. In 'Wet Panties' the city of Mumbai is shown to have grown economically advanced with skyscrapers and international schools but neglecting the self-respect of its women by missing out in incorporating the need for clean and well maintained public lavatories for them.

The stories showcase life in all its complexities, like in 'A Short Skirt', where a young girl is forbidden to wear a short skirt out on the streets due to the fear of ogling eyes and perhaps even a rape in future; but where, on those same streets, the bikshus in the name of religion walk in all their stark nakedness.

In this collection of my 20 stories, I have attempted to guide the reader to move through the different emotions of my country, locating the hearts of the characters and decide if they are different from anywhere else in the world. As after all, there is certainly something like universal brotherhood.

Ruby Malshe

A PLACE IN MUMBAI

Having completed her education in the city of Mumbai, Parveen had sort of got attached to this city of glitter. Popularly known as the Bollywood of India, this city of wealth and fame had a variety of people residing in her posh residences, bungalows, hutments and slums.

All throughout her student years, Parveen had lived at hostels attached to the educational institutions where she had studied, but now having completed graduation, she had no place to stay on and had begun to lookout for a paying guest accommodation. This had become a great cause of disappointment to her parents who had always hoped that she would return to her home town and who repeatedly urged her to return to her house in Gujarat.

Parveen's birthplace was Udwada, a small town in the city of Gujarat; a place visited just a few times in the year by the minority community of Parsees. It housed the great fire-temple, the Atash-Behram, most revered by these people with a Persian origin. The story told so far, stated that the fire worshiped by the Zarthostis in that Fire Temple was originally from Persia, which during the period of afflictions on the community had been secretly brought out by the worshippers who had hid it and brought it to the place their ship had landed in.

Actually those worshippers then, were not Parsees but the Zarthostis; who, when they had reached the western coast of India, were welcomed by the Indian kings as Parusis, which meant neighbours. The king of Gujarat had initially refused them any place on his land, saying that there was no place for any more people on that soil since it was already populated enough. The king it seemed, had shown those fair skinned people a glass of milk filled to the brim for them to understand the over populated condition of the place, but the cleaver Zarthostis had added sugar to the milk and instead explained, that they in fact would mix with the people of the land like sugar in the milk without any trouble, making the nutritional wealth of the milk flavoured with their sweetness. Perhaps the answer had impressed the king who had then allowed them to stay on, but with a condition that they would keep their religious faith secret and not ever try to convert anyone into it. Since then, the community had been known as Parusis, who later during the British invasion to India began to be pronounced as Parsis as the English men couldn't pronounce the Indian word correctly.

The community of these Parsis today was a dying community, as they had never let go of the promise given thousands of years ago to the Indian King. The dwindling numbers of the people of this community could probably be because they still didn't allow any conversions and also, many modern Parsi women and men were observed to be stepping out of the religious barricading of the sects fundamental beliefs due to inter-caste marriages.

It was not that Parveen didn't like her birth place; she in fact loved the calm, peaceful and tranquil atmosphere of the serene landscape, where people lived unruffled by any urgency of a city life. However, there was not much in that place that she could do for a living. Udwada was a small town even now, just as it had been in the olden days. The modern cities in India had changed so much, and yet Udwada didn't have much to boast about except its Fire Temple. If Parveen had to make a living for herself, there wasn't much scope for any aspiration in that place. All her learnings would have no applicability over there. In fact, no one really visited that place except with the purpose of religious sentiments. The few people who still had their family homes over there, had as if marginalized themselves to stay within the periphery of that place in peace unlike that of the modern cities, away from any competitive manner of living.

Her modern education had however taught her to compete. As a child she had participated in competitive races on the playground, as a student she had worked hard to score in competitive exams. Life in general outside her hometown had been a customary race she had to regularly run to catch up with living.

And so began her hunt for a paying guest accommodation and a job in the city.

"Search for a place where there is a young unmarried son. Trap him in your beautiful tresses and set his heart aglow with your smouldering eyes. He will plead for a life partnership and don't be in a hurry to foolishly reject the offer. Jump at it smoothly. You will get a permanent accommodation due to marriage, which otherwise will be next to impossible in this city. That's how cool it is."

Her friend's advice was indeed cunning but there was perhaps an element of truth in what they said; but marriage was the last thing at the moment on Parveen's mind. She had got a job offer as a receptionist in a three-star hotel at central Mumbai. On duty, her meals were taken care of and the income was good enough for a not very aspiring girl like her. So she began her search for a room in the vicinity of her work place, to stay on as a paying guest. She soon found one on a twin sharing basis, but the flat owner got greedy and added two more occupancies in the same room. It felt too cluttered and she didn't hesitate to go and speak to the land lady.

"Madam," she said approaching her, "You had agreed on only two of us earlier. Four people in one room are just too much in such a small place. It has begun to appear more like a dormitory with a bed and a side table for each one of us. One bathroom then, is also not sufficient. There is a lot of clashing and……." But the land lady didn't let her complete her complain list. Cutting her short she began quite angrily, "Only the two of you! For the amount you have agreed to pay me, I can't even buy myself a decent meal in this city. I hope you are abreast with the price hikes in everything around. I need you to understand that it certainly is not easy for an old lady like me to survive on that pittance you pay me as rent. If you are dissatisfied with the situation, I would suggest that you shift elsewhere."

That was like a metaphor for 'Get lost'. The search for another place began and soon she moved out to a bigger place, once again on a twin sharing basis but this time it was her room-mate who smoked till late, and the fumes chocked her. She couldn't risk her health with those betel leaf fumes. After all, passive smoking was supposed to be more dangerous than smoking itself. It was better to live crowded and long, instead of spacious and short. She once again decided to move out for a better environment.

To her bad luck though, she couldn't find any accommodation which would suit her purse and so she went back to the same four in one place she had initially left. Luckily that place was still vacant but the greedy old land lady now demanded a higher price from her. The welcome was tinged with a sarcastic tone. "I told you it was becoming difficult for a single lady like me and yet I was hesitating to increase your rent but then you decided to leave."

She knew that was being nastily polite. What she probably wanted to tell her was, 'You want more space, my foot. Take it or leave it. This is a punishment for your treachery.' Well, beggars couldn't be choosers and so she was back to square one.

Her family in Udwada was constantly in touch with her calling her back, but then Udwada could never have been able to give her a feel of Mumbai and Mumbai had this special honey like quality which attracted people like bees to her. This city was like a skin disease, which if it once attacked an individual, made it very difficult to do away with.

However, her job kept her going and she continued to live in the greedy lady's claustrophobic room. But she kept herself busy on the look-out for a place that would, she very positively assured herself, give her space to breathe freely.

After a few months of an intermittent search, she finally did find a place that suited her budget along with fulfilling her hopes. It was a room an old couple wanted to share in their home with someone they could trust and rely on and she luckily fit the bill. An icing on the cake was that the room even had a small balcony looking down at the street. She couldn't have asked for more.

Soon she moved in, thanking God for such a blessing. The old couple was also quiet and reserved and gave her the quiet space she had always longed for.

As she sat in the antic easy chair on the balcony with a modern ceramic cup of tea in her hand, the fumes of the hot liquid gave their warmth to her face as she put the cup to her lips. She turned to look inside the room to check if she had left the fan on. The old couple had nobody of theirs in this big world and they had assured her that she could stay there as long as she pleased. Though they didn't interact much with her and kept their distance, she could sense that they were quite happy that they had a paying guest who would make the payments on time as money was of course their basic need. But perhaps, she wondered, there was an even greater need that they had hidden from her; the need for a youthful presence that gave an assurance of help to them in their old age. She smiled, taking in a deep breath of understanding. Yes, she was young and strong to live alone in a big city like Mumbai but her parents too were old and probably they were missing her this moment. She turned once again to look inside the room from the balcony where now she had been relaxing for quite some time. First she took in the empty vastness of the room and then again looked out from the balcony into the crowded street below. All she could see was a place packed with excess, where men and vehicles were jostling for space to reach back home on time to someone waiting for them; to an unpretentious emotion of love; to a hub of genuine feelings.

A BUTTERFLY WILL REMAIN BEAUTIFUL

To some people, life without a mission would be like flotsam on the sea. A mission would sort of give some direction to their otherwise needless wondering. It would be like a push to a boat stuck in the mud on the coast to move on ahead in the cool flowing waters of the river of existence. The oars of some plans or a belief would then be like a motor engine added to that boat, giving speed and direction for the journey of life.

Kashti was in deep sleep when the phone on the side table to the right of her head had jerked her awake with its loud tune. Though it had been a tune from her choicest music albums, its ringing in the middle of her sleep had made it sound unpleasant. Of late Kashti hardly got the required number of hours to sleep and give rest to her mind and body. The little sleep that she managed to snatch in between work and stress, was not peaceful but disturbed with worrisome thoughts which didn't allow her to feel secure even in slumber. Her father had been a force in her life which made her feel protected, safeguarded and confident every moment. The sight of this great support himself on support systems was definitely scary. The picture of the ailing old man with pipes stuck into his body as life supports was therefore not easy to let go off, even when she returned home at night from the hospital to gather enough strength for the next day. Though no more a little child but a mature woman, the fear of losing her father was no less but instead multiplied every day as she sat by his side at the hospital bed. Her father's journey on earth had been a long and fulfilled one and perhaps his planet earth holiday plan had come close to its expiry date. Probably any day soon he would board the flight for his eternal existence and then she would never see him again. She belonged to a prayerful family which believed that there was indeed in reality, a land enchantingly beautiful, where there could never be any illness and neither any ill will of mankind. She was faithfully convinced by the scriptures, and believed that in that land the rivers would be filled not with water but milk; where every tongue would have the sweetness of honey, unlike some acidic tongues on earth. She had learnt that when the Lord had created the earth, He had made it a replica of His Heavenly abode; but man in his selfishness and greed was leaving behind ugly sights, spoiling its inherent pulchritude. Man had abused this planet beyond the normal measures of requirement, leaving behind the grimy remains of his avaricious emotions. She remembered how when as a young girl she had once returned home from school, angry and hurt due to the nasty behaviour of some friend turned enemy and mouthed vengeful words while empting out the contents of her school bag, her father then a young and robust man had held her close to his heart and wiping away her tears whispered the word 'forgiveness' in her ear. 'Forgiveness is a requisite for a place in heaven my dear' he had said and she had never forgotten that lesson. Now perhaps her dad was going to be moving on to that home in the skies that he had always spoken of. However, it was difficult to let go.

All the wise words of wisdom she had read time and again from the Holy Book couldn't cut off the cord of affection she had for her procreator. However old a child was, she could never cease to possess a childish affection; one would forever have for a parent.

Whenever she was not by his bedside, there was always a knot of fear gripping her tightly. 'What if dad moves on without me by his side?' The old man's condition didn't seem to be improving a bit and the ghost of death like a fearful monster kept staring at her all the time. The doctors had done their bit and divulged in their silence the hopelessness of medical science which in spite of reaching a great magnitude of cures could never compete with celestial powers.

"Please make my dad alright doctor. It has been so long now without him at home. It just doesn't feel nice there without him."

The doctor had turned and patted her shoulder with an understanding smile as if he wanted to tell her to better get used to the feeling.

****

As the phone rang, her muscles tightened in fright and she wondered if it was some message from the hospital.

"Hello", she spoke into the instrument. A rich accented voice spoke back to her.

"Good morning. Am I speaking to Miss. Kashti?"

"Yes, this is her."

"Miss. Kashti, this is Benvinita from the BBC channel. Mister Raj from the 'Heaven's Land Church' referred you to us. The BBC is working on a reverse missionary series and we are getting across to people from different countries for this purpose. We believe that you are a woman of faith and would be a good representative from India for the episodes we are developing to be telecasted in our next series. If this offer interests you, our group could come over and explain the details to you."

In her heart of hearts she knew that this was a life time opportunity that was knocking at her door; however, what she was unable to comprehend, was whether to scream out with joy at her luck or shriek in resentment at the time Lady Luck had chosen to visit her. It had been a dream of hers to spread the word of the Lord to all ears willing to listen, but how could she with a terminally ill father lying in the hospital, even remotely think of moving away from him and desire to cherish it. For a moment she was even upset with her Creator to put into her lap the opportunity for the fulfilment of her dream at a time like this. Digesting every word spoken to her, she wondered how the Lord too had failed to be His Omniscient self and blundered to make an error in time management.

Gulping down her disappointment she spoke back into the instrument.

"It's indeed a great honour madam to receive a call from you but I must say it has come to me at a wrong time in my life. My father is in the hospital and his condition is serious. I need to be more by his side than anywhere else in the world."

After having spoken to the voice at the other end, Kashti felt her eyes wanting to release a flood of emotion but at the same time she also felt relieved. She knew for sure that she had made the right decision. Her father was her world and how could she ever even think of leaving his side, especially at a time like this when he needed her the most and instead reach out to the world outside. Her world at the moment consisted of her father and her hopes were pinned on to his recuperation. The voice at the other end she could imagine didn't expect the answer it had received. The BBC was too prestigious to hear of a rejection from anyone anywhere in the world.

"Oh!" The voice seemed a bit taken aback. "I am extremely sorry Ms.Kashti to hear about your father." There was a pause. "Well, it was nice talking to you but you could if you please save our number? Perhaps you would like to speak to us when you feel more relaxed. Have a good day. We wish you all the best for your dad's quick recovery and hope that he gets well as soon as possible."

She knew that being more relaxed meant the time when her father would have completed his walk of life. 'What was life', she thought, 'but a tight rope-walk where the rope was tied to the two poles of existence; namely birth and death'.

As man climbed the pole of birth and placed his feet on the rope, his cautionary period began. As he lifted his arms raised up like in worship, he had to manage a balance and keep himself gripped safely from the swinging of pleasures, greed, pride and lust which could sway him too hard to his fall of character before he successfully reached the other pole of exit. As he walked this tight rope journey, his focus would inevitably be disturbed by words of encouragement to achieve the pride of success or the cries of ridicule bombing him in decision making wars which would shake his faith. As the walk of life progressed and gained momentum, cups of refreshing peace and love were held up to him from the harmonious cosmos of nature but the fears implanted in him by structured systems of human organisations often added stressful compositions of worthless weight and depression instead. Till finally one fine day, like always, it would all be over and the curtains would fall at the finale. Perhaps that's when all would be more relaxed.

She took a deep sigh of grief as she remembered the words; 'Life is full of sound and fury signifying nothing'.

'What could be her mission in this life?' she wondered. 'What could be every man's mission? What had been her father's mission?' It appeared to her as if all missions sailed speedily in the turbulent waters of the river of life. Every river had to meet a sea and every sea got submerged into an ocean. The flow of the waters looked enchantingly glorious from afar. The journey appeared refreshingly exciting. But alas! It always came to an end, bringing a tear to some eyes. Life was like a war which man fought to survive as long as he could.

But then Ruskin Bond came to the rescue of her grieving thoughts: 'And when all wars are done, a butterfly will still remain beautiful'. There was so much beauty in this gift of life in spite of its short span, she thought, smiling to herself.

A KEEP

Malhar came from a family which valued traditions. Traditions were like the security guards that made the residents of a colony feel safe from the burglars of modernity. Malhar too had had a very traditional upbringing and if not for his love story, he would have never thought of going against the customs and beliefs of his progenitors.

It certainly wasn't easy for him to go against the strength of the feelings of his family members. No one had ever dared to propose a love marriage at his home. It was something unheard of. Marriages at his place were a family matter and not just a narrative of love. Traditionally, Indians fell in love after marriage and not prior to tying the sacred knot. In fact, sometimes the couple wouldn't even have had an opportunity of see one another before their wedding night. However, times had changed; and yet at Malhar's home, the doors had been shut to the renovation of thoughts.

Of course Malhar loved Rajni. He certainly wanted to settle down with her as his life partner but she belonged to another caste and that was a major hurdle he would have to cross over to convince his parents, explaining to them that love had no understanding of any kind of boundaries; either of language, caste or creed. Actually Malhar feared being disowned by his family. His father had warned him that if he went against their wishes, he would have to wash his hands off the family property and business and that of course the young blood in him wasn't able to accept as a fair deal. Also, he respected and loved his parents, for after all what he was today was only due to their efforts and love for him.

"Malhar, the world is moving ahead in leaps and bounds. Whoever today believes in caste system? It's all so archaic. Why don't you open the doors of modern ideas to your family and make them understand that my entry in their house is in no way going to be harmful to them?"

"Rajni I agree with what you are saying but it's not all as easy as you make it sound. My parents had never known one another before they got married. In fact even at the time of their marriage they were total strangers. It's hard for such people to accept our modern ideas. If we push too hard we will only end up hurting them and ourselves."

"So what do you propose to do? Wait till they can look into your heart or feel the need to do so?"

"Please try to understand my situation Rajni, I belong to this family. I owe a lot to them. I just cannot take a hundred and eighty degrees turn and tell them that I don't value their thoughts nor respect their belief system. Yes, I know it's my life and I have every right to live it the way I want to, but that's not the way I was brought up to react. And what about my work, have you given that a thought? I am involved in the family business. If I act very revolutionary then I might be kicked out from my share of work and property and that wouldn't be fair to both of us. I hope you will at least agree with that? Rajni, my parents have put in a lot of hard work and have great hopes in me. I can't hurt them. I have to gradually convince them. It wouldn't be right on my part to simply walk out on them to get married to you."

****

Today Malhar didn't spend much time with her like the earlier days. Rajni could see that he was being torn apart between his new bride and her. It had now been a month since he had got married to Nirmitee, a beautiful young woman his parents had chosen to be their daughter-in-law.

In spite of his parent's anger and refusal to accept her as their daughter in law, Malhar had convinced her that things would someday soon, get sorted out and had urged her to step out of her parent's home and begin to live with him in a place that they together had purchased to make into a holiday home for their future. Live-in relationships then were the new mantra in a land that didn't want to let go of its old cultural inhibitions; and where its youth stubbornly and disobediently wanted to taste the forbidden fruit of passion.

Love made people blind, and Rajni had certainly suffered from short sightedness. Malhar's plans had injected an excitement into her and she had argued with her parents and stepped out of their home to spend the rest of her life with the man who had simply to hold her in his arms for her to feel comforted from all the anger her mum and dad had sensibly and justifiably aimed at her.

Rajni had begun to earn a living quite early in life. She was smart to look at and had a very shapely and beautiful body. Blessed with attention, she never had had any trouble getting herself modelling assignments. In fact model coordinators queued up to her with contracts to be signed.

A good amount of those earnings she had utilized in the house they had then begun to call a home for themselves.

His parents too had of course been very angry with him for what he had dared to do in spite of them telling him that they would never accept Rajni as their daughter-in-law, since she belonged to a different caste. Her mother had cried and gone sick and tired of trying to convince her against her plans of moving out. Her father had got very upset that his daughter was not to receive her rightful respect and position in her lover's family.

"Why are you behaving as if there are no other young men in the world? If you agree, we can start looking out for a good life partner for you." Her mother had expressed her concern once again. "This live-in thing is not accepted in our land. You will not get any respect for what you are doing to yourself. He is a man, and men always get away with everything in this world. Don't forget that it's a man's world."

She of course did get worried and scared when her mother spoke like that to her, but then there was some anger seething within her which hated to hear those words. If it was a woman who created man, then how could it be a man's world? What did they mean by saying that the world belonged to the men? If not for the women, where would these men be?

When Malhar and she had gone looking out for a place to move into, they both had agreed to equally share the expenses the place would demand. But today, as she sat waiting for him to come home, she understood that the expenses were not only monetary but also emotional; and these she now realized she had spent on more than him.

Their initial attraction had perhaps been too charged, and it had driven them towards each other even agreeing to share the joys of a couple without the chains of legality. After all, they were young and adventurous. Rajni was only twenty three and Malhar twenty six then. The next ten years literally had flown past at great speed. There had been so much freedom in the togetherness of the two. It had been a beautiful relationship, which had left no place for any demands or jealousies. If there was anything between the two who were deeply in love, it was only an abundance of caring and sharing.

Those ten years had been simply wonderfully comfortable, but now suddenly, she found herself sitting all alone on the double bed they had purchased from the Chor bazaar at a throw away price. The bed had at times creaked under the weight of their love making, but today it stood silent, watching her loneliness as she lay on it, wide awake at 1:30 a.m. thinking of those times gone by.

For ten years Malhar had kept trying to convince his parents about his love for her, but they indeed had been a stubborn lot. Their pressure had finally worked on him and he had relented to it. His wedding night had left her sick and depressed. She had gone too far on a journey with the man she loved, to now return home to her parents.

Today, her heart was like usual feeling the pinches of envy as she thought about Malhar being with his wife. Ten long years he had tried to make his parents accept her, failing which he had finally given in to their tantrums. His mother had cried and threatened her son with her life, successfully melting his heart to the taste of her desires. Yes, his parents had finally succeeded in convincing him to get married to their choice of a woman for economic and social benefits; and he had agreed. The girl was the daughter of a rich business partner of his father and most essentially she belonged to their same caste.

"How can you do that? We are as good as married. It's now ten years since we are living together as man and wife. Can't you explain to your parents such simple stuff? Or is it that you too are now quite changed and secretly want to leave me and are using your parent's desires as an excuse to get away? After all you are not a child. You are an adult and you can make your own decisions." She was fuming when he had announced to her the decision of his parents. But he had been quick in comforting her like always. "What's wrong with you? How can you even think that I have gone astray in our relationship? This marriage will just be for the namesake. I can't afford to let go of all the family property. After all for how long are we not going to begin a family? And our present monetary condition is not all that great to give all the right things to a child we surely must have someday soon. If you keep doubting me, how will I move on? I know that my parents are being quite selfish with their demands; if only they would accept you as my wife, we could be married and live in my parent's house, but this country has its roots too strongly tied up in the caste system to let its youth live free and new from the clutches of the painful chains of the old system."

Tonight Malhar was not with Rajni; she lay on the bed alone clasping the pillow tight to her chest and sobbed quietly into its soft cotton cover. Her thoughts had taken up a solo journey of fear, thinking of Malhar sleeping close to his new wife; the lawful one; his nose twitching and getting ready for a sneeze when her hair came in between their proximity. Perhaps he had already sneezed, but now when she retorted with a 'God bless you' she was jealous of the long life he would be spending with her.

The laws of the world had proclaimed them man and wife but all of a sudden those same laws had transformed her into a keep. For ten long years she had abstained from carrying that title because he too had equally been single.

As she sat alone, she wondered why she had erred in her careless youth to not insist on carrying out the legal obligations of a marital status. The same live-in relationship, which earlier didn't carry any fringes of attachments with it and flew high in the blue skies of freedom without any encumbrances, had suddenly begun to desire a string of attachment. It had certainly been a long probation period; ten years. My God! She thought to herself, she should have thought of permanency. She had experienced everything in this togetherness. Whether it had been love or emotional help or material support; she had seemed all the while all so sure and permanent, that she had felt no need for the space of even a single legal paper. But today, she wondered if she had been cheated.

The modern world had failed her. The court had missed a broader horizon, focussing on the narrow ancient thoughts. The term, 'wife' needed a broader and an expansive interpretation, beyond the thinness of a sheet of paper. Damn it! Ten years they had lived together as a husband and wife, and just because they hadn't signed important legal papers, they suddenly had become only a man and a woman?

Now those mental archaic dinosaurs called her his keep. All of a sudden! What a primitive world! She was never kept; she had contributed equally in this relationship. But in this last month, he had visited her like a man visited a prostitute. The nights he had been to her, had not in any way commercially benefited her and yet…..she was an independent working woman. In fact even today, her pay cheque had a larger figure printed on it. In fact it was much, yes, much more than what he received from the family business he was so scared to part with. It was that legal one, back at his other home, who was dependent on him and yet today, heads turned when she stepped out.

She wondered whether she must continue to hold her head up high, or bow it a bit in fear of the single grey streak which had begun to appear on it and which certainly reminded her of the time she had lost.

A STORM IN A TEA CUP

Arvind Pandit's day began early; as early as four in the morning. His body he felt had after so many years got accustomed to as little as the five hours of sleep that his work could let him have.

"Yes sir, you will enjoy this fresh lemon grass tea which I have made especially for you. Customers like you are God sent. Where would I be without people like you who love and appreciate the tea I make?"

As there wasn't much to hold Arvind back at home, he had left his father's house when he was very young. His father was a school master in a remote village of India, where the school consisted of a plastic chair, a plastic table stained by tea cup residues and a small black board hung on to the trunk of a tree. The tree being a banyan tree, gave a good amount of shade to the students who came there; of course, that was only if they got the time to attend the classes. Known popularly as Panditji, meaning the learned man; he certainly had earned a lot of respect in the village, but the tuition fees he received were a pitiable amount for anyone who needed money for a decent living. It was quite understandable that a village which lacked basic amenities like electricity, medical facilities and even a police station could easily become a hub of crimes and couldn't obviously have a crowd eager to improve themselves with learning. Yet Panditji was set on his learned principals of sharing what he could with those interested for the betterment of the village.

"Baba, for how long will we go on like this? This poverty has robbed me of my mother's love. If only we had the money baba, mother wouldn't have left us. This place doesn't even have a decent hospital till date. There is nothing we can get in this village. It seems to be a good for nothing kind of place. Why can't we simply move on to some other place that will respect us as human beings?'

Arvind had come to gradually understand from his father that money was not always a priority for all people. But when things began to get worse, he couldn't hold himself back any more and therefore one night impulsively, he moved on without looking back. He took a train to explore his future, and landed at the Dadar station in the city of Mumbai, where he got sort of stuck up for what it seemed to him now for eternity. To his good luck the moment he landed at the station, a young lad of sixteen, famished with hunger and troubled with poverty, he was picked up by an old tea stall owner who took him in charge due to materialistic reasons since he was in need of an errand boy without any obligations to pay him a stipend for the contribution of work he would put in. Arvind too was thankful for small mercies. A roof over his head was indeed a blessing most wanted by an immigrant.

Time moved on and making tea soon became Arvind's forte and the tea stall owner having no family of his own was glad to have found the young lad or else who would he have left his business to, after he moved on? One fine day he very generously made matters legal by putting in Arvind's name as an heir to his small property which was after all a big thing for a lad who had run away from his village in search for life in a place which was a man eats man kind of world. It was unbelievable that Arvind had found a Godfather in the foreign world; but to his sorrow, God gave and took away his gift too soon. His Godfather died one night, of a cardiac arrest.

Since then Arvind's life took a turn of responsibility. He even wrote to his father back in the village.

"Baba, I wish that you would come to Mumbai. I feel very lonely without you. Surely, you too must be missing me a lot? Your silence can't hide your feelings from me. I know that I did hurt you by moving away without informing you, but tell me, would you have allowed me to explore my life? There is no life in that place we call our home Baba. Mumbai throbs with living. It has welcoming arms and hugs for all.

The old man though was quite laid back and preferred a life walking on the grass and resting under trees. Arvind was left to wonder as to how anyone could love poverty so much to be satisfied with it and stay rooted in it. The least that he could do then was to send him some money regularly for his survival and sometimes a bonus of some books which he thought the old man would like to read and add to his existing knowledge.

He had after the demise of the stall owner made some attractive changes at the stall, decorating it with bottles of spices to make strongly flavoured cups of tea and had added two more stoves to make them a total of three, to brew the drink for the speeding travellers; some of whom had become friends with him due to their regularity.

"Yes sir, which flavoured tea would you like to try? I have over here cardamom, orange, lemon grass, mint and the regular masala tea. The weather being warm, the mint would be the best. Would you like to try a cup?"

The job was quite demanding, as it began very early in the morning and went on till late into the night keeping him on his toes. The people in Mumbai were tea lovers and anytime here become a tea time for the rich as well as the poor.

Of late though, he had heard some interesting news; that the parliament had decided to glorify the product of his job and elevate it to a position of glory giving it the place of pride as a national drink. Some of his educated customers had smilingly told him while sipping on the hot brew that his tea would probably be at par with the lotus and the Bengal tiger as a national symbol.

"Arvind you will be surprised to know that this drink you are serving us daily is no ordinary one and that it has caught the attention of many who feel that it needs a place of importance."

Mr. Agarwal who never missed Arvind's masala chai had in fact googled a search on his latest mobile phone and very informatively told him about how India was the fourth largest tea exporter in the world next to only Sri Lanka, Kenya and China.

But Arvind was quite puzzled at the development of such importance to be given to the most common drink of the common man. He wondered how a simple cup of tea could have varied shades and tastes of complexity right from the mountains of Darjeeling, Munnar and Nilgiri, till the plains of Assam. With its' variety of kind, he was sure that a rivalry about the honour would surely proceed after a competition of such kind.

At night though, before his eyes shut for rest, his thoughts lingered on this small stall, which had since years now become a place of business as well as a place of rest for him. He wondered whether his stall would get a share of the prize of fame, and whether his status, that of an ordinary chaiwalla would get a boost of national importance too. If things really took a positive turn, he would at least stand a chance to bring a smile of pride on the lips of his old man. It would be an amazing national success in a small tea cup.

Next morning when Mr. Agarwal came to the stall for his usual cup of tea before taking the train to work, Arvind began a conversation, "Agarwal bhai, as you mentioned yesterday about the promotion of this product, do you think that when this tea will get a lift to a superior position, it will lift along with it us chaiwallas too, or will we simply remain battling in a storm of existence in our tea cups?"

Mr. Agarwal after taking a sip from the cup licked his lips and smiled. His train had arrived and he hurriedly put the tea cup down and rushed towards the platform. "I'll give you the money for it tomorrow." He shouted looking back in his rush and disappeared in the crowd.

A VISIT TO THE WIDOW

Shagufta sat still with Amar in her lap. How would she manage to convince him that his father was never going to return home from office today? He had left home as usual this morning with a grey shirt unbuttoned till mid-way with the tie hanging loose round his neck and the black coat slung across his shoulder. She hadn't bothered to ask him what time he would return as he was never late. It had been six years since she had been married to him and he was a good man. He hadn't supplied her with any great emotional or fleshly ecstasies but she was quite contented with the relationship which had helped life to go on peacefully without any stress of big desires of achievements or happenings. She was a satisfied woman. Small joys gave her great contentment. The sun rising in the morning, idli dosa for breakfast, a nap in the afternoon and taking her three year old son to the garden in the evening before Rajdeep returned at seven sharp, were activities enough in her time-table to live happily in peace.

Today Rajdeep wouldn't knock the door at seven. The informers from his office had already passed on the news to her. He had suffered a fatal stroke. She wondered why Death had chosen to strike him. He was young and fit. There were so many old, unwanted and uncared for white heads suffering in the geriatric wards at several hospitals, but perhaps Death didn't like the smell of their poo in their adult diapers.

Night came on too heavily on her. It had never been this dark before. Normally, she was quite contented with the moon light that filtered in through the open windows but tonight she had kept the night lamp on. When the stars began to disappear, there was no need for her to wake up as she had not slept in the first place. She turned to see Amar who was fast asleep by her side. The child looked so peaceful in his ignorance of what had passed by since the day before.

It was time the milkman came to deliver the bottles of milk at her door. When the doorbell rang she left the bed lazily straightening her hair with her hands to look presentably better the first thing in the morning. But today besides the milkman, there was someone else standing there too; she could feel its presence.

It was Death which stood at her door invisible to her eyes and speaking to her, using her voice of silence.

"Though men feel that I cheat the life out of them, I am honestly impartial in my work. I take no sides and only do my work with due respect to the responsibility laid on me. I don't understand why any man must have any reason for complaint, as in fact I gift him the priceless gift of silence. I am not even harsh all the time and if at all I appear to be harsh, it is because some shallow men in their wish to blast my arrival make my sweet tongue appear instead, a tongue of poison when they spill a pool of blood blowing up human bodies in masses because of their religious differences. Otherwise, I prefer to come slowly and softly by surprise to relieve the dead from the trials of living."

As Shagufta looked on glassy eyed listening to the voice of Death, Life stood by her to speak on her behalf. She was a little nervous due to the presence of the two opposing strong forces besides her. She shut the main door with her elbow as she carried the milk bottles in her hands to keep them in the kitchen. Moving to the kitchen, she glanced into the bedroom to check if Amar was still asleep. She had to be ready before they brought Rajdeep's body home for the final farewell. His brother and family had gone to the office to take him from there to the hospital and were with him since then, and in fact they had told her not to rush anywhere but stay at home till they arrived. She was quite rightfully angry with Death. Seeing her anger, Life spoke on her behalf to her sister Death.

"I have till now in this house, worn the crown of pride in the breath of living and you suddenly come in giving me a rude shock, dethroning me of all my significance. You leave me in a state of confusion. Till now I was dancing on the string of breath to the rhythm of breathing and you simply came in uncalled for and snapped at the string as if nothing mattered, nor ever will. For you the cup of everything holds an empty space of nothing."

Shagufta was amazed at the two siblings of existence standing face to face arguing their positions. She was so used to peace in her house that she didn't like any form of chaos and so she intervened to stop their battle of words.

"Oh sisters of this universe, why do you fight so? You alternately occupy the home of the human bodies. To complete the circle of reincarnations you keep alternatively shifting yourselves. The human world has accepted you both but why are you so confused at the joys and the grief of these humans at your arrivals and departures?"

Life and Death both became silent listening to this young widow who appeared to them so passively accepting them. They had sort of got used to screams of joy and wails of pain; but this still and quiet woman was a puzzle they were not able to solve. But Death still had a larger problem to confront.

"In this nation of great spiritual insights, every guest is raised to the position of the Lord; 'Atithi Devo Bhava'— they proclaim the guest to be the Lord Himself and yet when I arrive to visit my sister Life, they make me feel most unwanted and unwelcomed. At the slightest announcement of my entry, every man rushes to some private or public alters asking for an extension on the life line to hold on to breath – the symbol of living. Ironically, in a state of his spiritual unconsciousness, he has continued to breath like a child, playing hide and seek under coverlets of comfort as if he were playing a game with my sister Life, under the cover of ignorance of the final moment till I arrive.

With technological advancements he tries to trick me to extend the stay of my sister by holding on to her with machines. How insulted I feel. This really makes me mad. Why can't this man accept my presence? It frustrates me when I am made to keep waiting till the machines are pulled off. I too have my particular choices; who are they to question me the reason why I choose them over another? I visit some earlier than the others, but that shouldn't make any difference as I have the whole of the body of mankind on my visiting list. They are partial to me, these men they play games with me. I know they like my sister more than me because she cheats their intelligence with the dazzle of the stones they call diamonds. My honesty they can't accept, and so sometimes I have to come so all of a sudden without giving them any time to even hear my approaching footsteps or notice my shadow. Then they feel I am like the tiger on the prowl striding past fields to eradicate my beautiful sister. Thinking that I am ugly, they keep wearing the different attractive and coloured garments of my sister Life on their perishable bodies. But they do not know that their neglect of me does not make me non existential. They fool themselves with the imaginary hope of eternity of their bodies. They push me far behind in their busy lives almost forgetting me and ignorantly believing that their bodies are going to be everlasting."

Life was feeling too proud as her sister Death was angrily expressing the impression she had set for herself in the world of men. She stood there in all her beauty, combing her silky hair, curling them at one moment and straightening them the very next. She had a box of colours beside her and she made use of them to beautify her body, smiling slyly at her sister who appeared pale and dark in comparison to her brightness.

Death was indeed upset and continued. "Her sticky glue of excitements and fun covers up the spiritual wisdom of most men with the coat of ignorance, leaving them to bask in the pride and glory of their false superiorities. Behind the heavy woollen cloaks of ignorance buttoned all the way up with shiny buttons of wealth and health, they hide the shirt of reality locked behind, till amidst the din of their living they suddenly hear the knock of the worst bell on their dear ones heart. And then they get so upset with me, and scream 'How could it be so!' Though in shock, they do not hesitate to angrily express their displeasure. 'We were given no forewarning. What a rude guest. How shocking Death is.' What audacity they have. They call me shocking when I myself am shocked at their amnesia about their real destination and instead have got so absorbed in their holiday home; this earth."

Shagufta couldn't bear Life being insulted by Death in her presence. She stepped forward boldly to confront Death with her reasoning.

"What do you mean by amnesia? Your reality is so cruel that people here certainly prefer to forget even if temporarily, your lurking presence. We humans have no shock absorbers to stand strong at your arrival. We either break down or go dumbstruck due to your awe inspiring arrival. You simply barge into our peaceful life of pleasant forgetfulness and leave us dumb founded.

And look at me now. Look carefully. In spite of the terrible fate you have served me with, I have faced your bullet of everlasting pain with my ammunitions of fear and loneliness with a strength perhaps that even astonishes you." She faced Death angrily. "You have left me a widow and my child fatherless. My life was so much on a comfortable driveway and suddenly you put brakes on it. I have no shock absorbers and I am completely shaken up. You are an awe inspiring visitor. You have barged into my peaceful life of pleasant forgetfulness and left me dumb founded."

Death was quite amused at her sudden outburst, for till now she had accepted her quite calmly. She never had thought that there was so much angst seething inside this young lady.

"I thought you had finally accepted me with a calm mind. Everywhere I go there is a lot of crying and wailing but with you, there was so much silence that I mistook it for a greater understanding; but now I can say that you too are not different. My arrival has numbed you and your silence is the result of that numbing. I can understand your feelings on survival which my arrival has thrust upon you."

"Survival! It's a battle you have put me into." She snapped at Death instantly. "And to face the situational pain you have inflicted on me, the only ammunitions I have to fight this battle are fear and loneliness."

"My dear, I have not come to hurt you or your child. The Lord has His peculiar ways of feeding you with His love. Don't forget that He is watching you every moment. If you lose out on the spiritual ecstasy in this quagmire of earthly stings which keep leaving bruises on your spirit due to your focus only on your lost joys, then you will leave untouched the beyond without even a glimpse at it, though you will never be able to say that an opportunity was not given to you. The choice is yours my dear. It has been whispered to you in your heart. Either you accept this moment of your loss and feel totally stranded or take it as an opportunity to fill up the lull in your life with His remembrance in the silence of your heart. If you take the normal route you will remain ignorant of His presence within you like most people do and instead go on filling it up with noises of superficial happiness but if you choose the other route, you will gain an insight into a totally new consciousness."

From the stillness of her body language Death it appeared, had successfully convinced her that there were no losses in existence. Things just were like the philosophy of 'It Is'.

Softly she then spoke to the dark sister, "What can I do? They wail and cry so loud disturbing my peace. They simply do not allow me to forget. In their horribly chilling cacophony, the voice of my conscience loses its clarity."

Now it was Life's turn to express her thoughts, "This is a cruel world. It lives in an ignorant inquisitiveness and can't help to let the desires that flood its heart lie low. This world consists of the ignoramus who can't understand that the worldly suffering needs a quiet place and therefore they keep disturbing the victim left behind to suffer when the deceased has left. I am the one they desire." She turned to her sister Death and continued, "You are the unwanted. There is no place for you or your philosophies on this planet. All your greatness only the dead can understand and appreciate. But they are tongue tied; so how will they explain their gained wisdom to those you have left behind with me? I am too mesmerizing for them to let go of me. After all, my fair skin, colourful eyes, silky hair and palatial apartments, can't be not attractive; what have you got to offer for the attraction you ask for?"

Death stood quiet, listening to her sister and turned to look at Shagufta. She looked so helpless in between the power of the two extremes of life. With her voice filled with emotion the young widow spoke softly.

"Visitor after visitor keeps coming to meet me. Some of them are just acquaintances. They do not even really know me. All these six years since I have been living over here they have never spoken to me and yet now they crowd my house as if it is their duty to disturb my emotions as rightful neighbours residing in the edifice of humanity. Last year Rajdeep had got hit by a car and we had even had to hospitalise him. It was hell to manage the house, him and the kid, but at that hour of my need they never came to share any responsibility of mankind and now that he is not there they have all come dressed in whites. Some of them even glare at me because I am not wearing white, but then I have no time to go and purchase a pure white. In our tradition, young brides have a colourful wardrobe; blacks and whites are considered inauspicious. I never in the remotest of my thoughts thought that I should have kept one white at least, for any emergency."

Death instantly spoke in between her thoughts. "That's exactly what I mean when I say that my sister Life grips your senses too tightly for you to think beyond the colours of joy."

But Shagufta continued to speak ignoring Death, "Now they express worry about my single existence in this tragically multifaceted huge world, almost forcing me to feel lost in this moment. They ask me questions like, 'How will I continue to live all alone and how I will bring up my child without a father?' They attack my ears with a battalion of questions not realizing that my ears have gone deaf with shock. I say nothing. I have no answers at this moment. How can I know the future? If I had known it, would I have allowed you to come and ruin my life?"

Death raised her eyebrows at the lady's verbal insult to her but went on to explain to her grieving soul the need to stay calm.

"Oh my dear, they don't mean any harm to you. They themselves are in a state of shock which has scared them. In the heart of their hearts they worry if I were to select any of their homes for my next visit. What are you so worried about such sad souls? In their usual bored life they regularly crowd sites of flimsy thrills. Movies, spas, dinners, are the regular places they gather at to while away their time, but now with your loss, they have simply made a change in their programme. It's like they have had enough of wacky fun and now they want something serious. They visit you now to know what happens when I, the dreaded visitor arrives. Your house at this moment is the perfect spot to understand sorrow. All the institutions of the world have got so grossly involved in the triviality of fun, that they miss out on the lesson of acceptance. And from time to time, pain or its understanding is needed like a medicinal puff used by an asthmatic patient who will otherwise go out of breath. Imagine, just last night you were a bride and now look at you. Yes, you are not wearing the traditional white but yet your pale look covers up the need of that colourless material. Just a look at you scares them; all those who till now were so engrossed in their incessant nonsensical laughter mocking me. Now they have through you, got a glimpse into my terrifying aura and are scared of the pain you are going through. The drama of life has suddenly changed a scene, and they like an audience have flocked to the theatre of your home."

Now it was Life's turn to express the insignificance of the role of her sister Death in spite of the fear she injected into many hearts.

"My dear sister, I agree that your presence is too terrifying for man to digest easily; but yet, if only you were to look carefully, you would notice that the lady is just the same as she was before. Your taking away her life partner is not the same as taking away her life. I continue to live in her, and she will soon forget your wounds inflicted on her heart. Though from time to time, remembrance will certainly bother her. All those who today have flocked to see her, if you were to notice, are quite disappointed as they see no real big difference in her; not a very notable one at least."

Shagufta had not eaten anything since last night. She was feeling weak and fed up of the jostling of the words between Life and Death. She somehow felt as if neither of them mattered. She walked slowly to the bedroom and sat beside her sleeping child. Existence was like a big plate with a variety of delicacies spread on it. A few coloured vegetables, a piece of meat and some salad and if one was yet unhappy with the spread, it didn't really make a big difference to the décor of the plate. She had to stop the sisters from going on to prove their positions of importance.

"Yes, Life is quite right when she says that nothing really has changed. I continue to live even when the man in my life has ceased to exist. Look here,......" she turned to show them her beautiful house and continued, "The dining table and the chair stand facing one another just like they did when Rajdeep had left for work yesterday morning, the clock on the wall continues to tell the time, the shower in the bathroom I am sure will wet my hair like always and the iron will surely erase the creases on the crumpled clothes." She touched her face with her left hand, since with the right she was tightly holding on to the tiny fingers of Amar, as if she was somewhere deep down worried of losing him too. "This pimple on my face still bothers me, like it did on the day of my marriage. Oh how I kept touching it, hoping that it would vanish before Rajdeep would kiss me." Sighing softly she whispered to herself. "But now he will never kiss me." And then she was loud again. "Since last evening when I got the news of his passing away I have not eaten anything and now my stomach is shouting with the pangs of hunger. It's not that I didn't go to the kitchen at all. Amar had to be taken care of but I just didn't feel like putting anything in my mouth. It was as if my whole body had become full with sad news leaving no place for any food in it."

Her in-laws had by now arrived with Rajdeep's body. The dead body of the man lay in the middle of the living room. People too had gradually come in one by one to pay their last respects. She had woken up her child and washed him and put on fresh clothes on his tiny body and now she sat with him in her lap on the ground silently watching Rajdeep's still face. The same face had in the last six years revealed to her so many emotions of life, but now it lay still, stuffed with cotton buds in the nostrils. She wanted to rush up to him and pull out those buds and tell him to start breathing; but how could she have done that, they would have thought her to be mad. So she sat quietly resting against the wall just thinking nothing, as all round her, there were muffled sounds of crying.

"And now to add a topping to my emotional and physical pain, these people have all landed up here to catch something different in me and when they fail to lay their hands on any concrete difference, they wag their tongues like little, helpless puppies who lick their masters feet and nobody really knows whether they do so because it gives them a feeling of safety and security, or they do it to make their masters feel fine. They have now assumed that there is a vacuum in my life and they keep offering some unwanted assistance and in fact some of my very close friends even cry on my behalf. I don't really understand why my tears have dried up. Perhaps they have understood that it makes no sense wasting them self now. But none of these people are going to take me to their homes to make me a part of their families, none of them will share their husbands with Amar even when he is too young and needs a father figure."

Amar was seated in her lap and looked quite remorse with the environment of sorrow. He actually wanted to go to the garden. Since last evening his mother had not taken him out to play with his friends and he just sat in her lap playing with her dupatta, twirling it around his little fingers, unaware of his earthly loss. He appeared sad because his mother was not happy. He did not know that he would no more have his dad to take him out to a film or to buy him an ice-cream or to attend the open day in his school, or pick him up when he fell down or have a race with him and lose in the run, to give him the joy of winning. He did not know that he would have to manage all these simple physical tasks and fill up the easy duties of day to day living all alone holding the frail hand of his mother who would be loaded with an emotionally heavy heart. He saw so many guests coming to greet his mother. They sat by her side and wept sad tears. They appeared like hypocrites on a one day sympathy picnic. They talked and spoke of the past, stating facts of the old times, digging up her lost memories as they couldn't bear to see her stability in spite of her loss and made attempts to toss her off balance. And as they went on and on, they perhaps forgot that Death was spying on them; keeping a close watch on them with a conceited smile as she circled a date for them on her calendar.

IN SILENCE, THE WIDOW RETURNS

The house was filled with the pleasant perfume of incense sticks and the tranquil sound of prayers. Whether these did benefit the dead or not, Shagufta did not know, but they did give the environment a feeling of purity and a charged atmosphere to the surrounding. Thirteen days had passed since Rajdeep had moved on in his journey leaving her behind and his son in her charge all alone. Actually she was by now getting quite used to it; though sometimes she did miss out on an affectionate hug and a passionate kiss. Monetarily there was no problem; though Rajdeep had been the only earning member, he had arranged the finances very wisely leaving his small family untroubled and satisfied for their daily requirements. Troubles though, yet visited her, but only from the emotional gateway and sadistically they kept playing with her heart and at times even pushed her to the periphery of tolerance when Amar kept demanding for his father. How could she bring back the one who had left? How could she convince her child that everything would be fine in spite of the family suddenly becoming incomplete? The toy factories with their technological advancements had made so many robotic toys but she wondered why no one had yet thought of creating a robotic parent toy to fill up the space in the moment of a sudden departure of the real one where an unexpected vacuum was created by the wrath of the Ruling Energy. Perhaps it would be the privilege of some future generation to enjoy that sort of a heart convincing invention.

These thirteen days of house arrest had made a difference in her thinking though. The initial shock of her loss had dried up her tears, but as the days had passed by, the difference in her life and loneliness had showed its presence to her, making her alert to the widowed existence which couldn't be overlooked and yet in that loneliness she had got the company of wisdom which had filtered into her heart through the opening which the loss had made over there. This was her individual and personal achievement and it was difficult to be communicated to the others who hadn't yet been polished with grief. Her tongue stood still in her mouth unable to communicate and share what she had learnt; and even if she were to do so, how would anyone have got any wiser with her wisdom?

The society had chalked out thirteen days of a religious time table which she had followed step by step; but now that the days specially occasioned for sorrow were over, she wanted to move out at least for the sake of her child. Her in-laws too who had by their grieving presence filled up the empty space in her house, had now left to go back to their normal routine of living, leaving her once again all by herself to continue to live with the memories of their son. It was now only Amar, her three year old son and she that moved about in the physical dimensions which appeared far larger than they did when Rajdeep had been around. In fact there had been a time when they had felt the need for a larger apartment assuming that their family would grow with time. But destiny perhaps had other plans. Truly, life was too short a trip to gather a lot of belongings on the way. Lessening out on the needs instead of accumulating them was something every soul had to learn. In life, one needed to really cut out on things and not add on, in order to understand its significance, and to her benefit some all-powerful energy had done that great work for her though it appeared too cruel to digest. Life needed to be smooth and soft and well-cooked, but Death had left its raw imprint on it; like the raw salad in a plate of spicy and juicy meat. Though considered a wealth of health, it fell weak in contrast to the richness of its companion—the meat. Most palates relished the meat which in fact caused harm to the body and threw away the salad which gave more wholesomeness to their physical structure.

Amar who had given her company in her sorrow with his incessant questions about his father, was by now quite fed up of not receiving any concrete answers and was in fact quite angry with his father who had gone away on an official task without kissing him good-bye; and to top it all he was not even available on the telephone. His little body by now longed for some exercise and play which it used to get daily in the garden where he ran up and down the slides, felt butterflies in his tiny stomach when the swing went soaring up into the sky, and enjoyed the colour of the earth on his clean clothes when he rolled in the mud with the earth bucket and spade in his hand. Today he was very much ready and happy since it was after so many days that his mother had decided that it was not his fault that his papa had not returned home and had promised to take him out of the four walls of his home.

As she walked with him to the garden, she held his hand tighter than she used to do earlier. Perhaps it was an unconscious backlash of fear which made her hold on tightly to life. The string of breath had broken off so suddenly in Rajdeep when she had least expected it to. Tearing apart the façade of her husband's security around her, Death had actually ripped open her joy, separating it from her heart due to some emergency in the spiritual world unknown to her.

As she moved past the known faces which she greeted regularly every evening in the garden, she could sense them holding on to their breath. She wondered why they did that, and once again she had no answers. But she felt like a melodramatic queen on a parade in the green grass. The garden which always had looked beautiful to her today looked grey and dull. Almost everything around resembled the tragic pyre which had burnt up her husband's body.

How angrily the hungry flames had risen to eat up Rajdeep's body. It had been shocking to see the insignificance of the flesh in nature. A great part of her heart and its desires too had got burnt on the same pyre and probably because of their burning up; the flowers today in the garden didn't attract her attention to their mesmerising colours. She had been awe struck with the climax the creator of the universe had introduced in the performance of her happy life, leaving her with wonder at the sudden change of scenes.

And yet Amar had never looked happier to her than this particular day. She had clutched him so tight for the last thirteen days that perhaps he had felt a relief when his lungs had finally got an opportunity to breathe in freedom. As he played in the mud she sat beside on the coloured bench looking at him and wondering at his innocent ignorance of the cruelty of life. Other mothers who earlier used to sit and chat away their frustrations of regular living with her, today sat away whispering in their small groups from where she had deliberately stayed away this day. Some of them smiled at her when their eyes met and some moved their lips to express an apology. She simply nodded and smiled back wondering why people said they were sorry to someone who had lost a dear one. They certainly weren't responsible for causing any grief to the suffering one, then why did they take the blame?

Perhaps they now felt that her burden was too colossal and therefore felt inferior to her in their petty troubles of regular irregularities. She smiled at herself and her mind then suddenly began to talk to her.

'It's not a big deal. People come and go just like they do in this garden. In likewise manner Rajdeep came as a stranger to meet you, became a friend and then took on the role of a husband and look at that beautiful son of yours he has gifted you with before departing. And then just the way he came, he parted. A particular chapter in the book of your life is done and there is nothing to be sorry about it. You must keep reading the book and be absorbed in it. When you will come to the end of the pages, there will be certain chapters you will be so attached to, that you will never forget them and some chapters will be lost as probably they didn't have any significant material for your memory to hold on to.

Reading by itself is a joy and a lovely experience. As you read the book the characters on its pages take your attention in their grip but you are too smart to get attached to them. You move on from characters to characters and from book to book without any attachment to them and if you didn't, you would be crazy. What has happened to your smartness now while you are reading your own life? You need to move on. Put down the book with the sad ending and pick up a new one which will make you happy to balance your emotions.

These people who come to apologize to you are actually at a loss for words. They are going through an emotional bankruptcy. They have not got the wisdom Death has gifted you with and therefore they are sort of ashamed at their ignorant selves and apologize for the same. Your status is now naked. You have been stripped off your husband's attachment and they are unable to understand this half status of yours. They can't imagine your room without Rajdeep; they can't bear the thought of you sleeping soundly without his snoring disturbing you as they continue to cover their ears to stop the loud disturbing noise of their other halves when they would give anything for some peaceful rest; they can't imagine your face being untouched by a kiss which only expresses a lie of eternal relationship. You have faced the truth of life and they are yet entangled in its lie.'

The voice had now done with the communication and she smiled at the women gathered in groups around her. Continuing to smile at their curiosity she got up to leave. It was now time to return home. She had been out for too long. The evening sky was displaying a colourful picture and she sought Amar's attention to it. "Look Amar, look at the beautiful sky before it becomes dark. Come let's go home and watch it even better from our window. I'll give you the box of colours and a big paper to draw and capture it for your collection." The child was a lover of art and therefore quickly packed up his earth bucket and spade to exchange it for a paint brush. Amazingly he himself wiped his hands on his pants and got up to hold his mother's, leaving no reason for her to tell him to hurry or give him any promises for another day.

As she walked away past the other groups of women holding the hand of her child, she nodded at them with an understanding of their fears. If she were to say anything more than a hello or a bye, she would scare them with her words of experience and so she simply moved on in silence.

CONTRACT

Illness had changed Shusmita's perspective of life. A sudden cessation had come over a life full of fun involving ephemeral delight and travel which had given her umpteen opportunities for sight-seeing. With Ravi's health suddenly taking a dip for the worst, life had as if suddenly become for her a house arrest, where she had to constantly keep a watch on her husband's food intake and medicines which she believed would help improve his health. Actually, there had been nothing particularly wrong with Ravi; in fact he had always been a fit man and since his job involved a lot of travelling he had often taken her along with him. But that was only after his darling daughter Prajakta had left the nest empty, after he had got her married to a diamond merchant, Mr. Jasraj's son Amar.

Earlier when Prajakta had been a little school girl, Ravi's travelling most of the time was by himself, except during the school holidays when his wife and daughter were a delightful company.

"Sushmita, I wish you and Prajakta could accompany me on all my business trips. My work would then become pleasure and I would have no worries about leaving the two of you alone."

"I know Ravi, but Prajakta has school, and it is impossible to make a child travel with all her studies and school assignments; and besides too much of travelling would exhaust her as she is still quite small and frail. In any case we do come along with you during the school holidays, don't we?"

His work often took him to Mumbai, the coastal city of stardom. It was a city that spent a lot of money for things not worth a pittance. It was the Bollywood of fake glitter. Every time he returned home to Pune, he had a lot to share and tell his wife about the people of that glamorous city; its wealth, and its charm, but somehow he always felt that his family was safe and comfortable in their lavish apartment in Pune. Their house was a beautiful pent house in a small five storey building. It was like a little heaven on earth.

"That city Sush, is mind blowing. It throbs with a very different kind of energy. It's lovely to visit it for shorter periods of time but to settle down in that vibrant place......
......I think Pune is much calmer and soothing a place and our house is a miniature kingdom of bliss after all."

Since business often took him to Mumbai, he had at one time shared with his wife Shusmita, his desire to purchase an apartment in that glittering city to make his stay over there during his trips, more comfortable and more over it would be a good investment and also make him feel more at home with a place of his own.

"Sush, what do you say about purchasing an apartment in Mumbai? After all, my work keeps taking me there quite often and I spend quite a lot on the hotel stays there. A place of our own would certainly be a better deal and it would also be a good investment for our future."

She remembered very clearly how, when it was Prajakta's summer vacation at school, that they had gone house hunting to the present sixteenth most expensive city in the world. But they had been lucky as in those days things were more affordable.

Today as she remembered that purchase, she thanked her husband's farsightedness. "You do go there often but every time your stay is only for a day or two. You could easily go to your Suresh mama's house for such short business trips. You surely wouldn't be a burden to him as you would be out at work the entire day, returning only at nights to sleep and you could always give him some monetary token of appreciation which I am sure he would be looking forward to." She was right in a way, as his Suresh mama was a retired man who often suffered shortage of funds due to the growing price hikes in everything.

Suresh mama was a bachelor and lived in the suburbs of Mumbai in a one room apartment and he always looked forward to Ravi's visits as he loved some company in his otherwise lonely life. In fact he often urged Ravi to bring along his wife and daughter too. Ravi too, always politely assured him that he would do so someday but knew too well that the life style he had given his family in Pune was far too superior to adjust in a one room apartment in Mumbai.

The place he had focused on for purchase at that time was not in a posh locality, but his business acumen had told him that it would undoubtedly become unaffordable within a decades time with the rising prices of the city residencies.

However with time, Ravi gradually lost interest in work due to his failing health and since his work involved a lot of travel which now seemed to tire and exhaust him, he thought it best after a lot of reasoning with himself, to go in for an early retirement. The doctors had no authentic or satisfying response to his deteriorating health as all his reports showed him to be absolutely fit and fine.

"Mr. Ravi, you need to take life easy. You have for quite some time done a lot of running around. I understand your work requires you to do so, but in the bargain, your body and mind have taken a beating. It's time you think of an early retirement." Turning to Sushmita he continued, "What do you think Mrs. Rai? There is nothing medically wrong with Mr. Ravi, he just seems to be mentally overstressed and you know a tired mind can harm the body."

So the only probable answer to his not feeling too well was then blamed on to his earlier lifestyle, which had to a certain extent involved hurry, worry and the curry syndrome that could be now without any hesitation held responsible for his present condition. Thankfully, his wise investments were enough to sustain the medical and other expenses of the family and help them to carry on respectably in spite of his not replenishing the coins further.

Prajakta had by then grown up into a beautiful young girl of marriageable age. The powers above had showered grace on his family and their darling daughter had got married into an honourable family of a diamond merchant. With their daughter well settled, Ravi's health once again had begun to show improvement and Shusmita thought that perhaps her husband's earlier ill health had been due to a subconscious stress due to a lot of strain and tension for his family. Everything once again seemed to have got into shape and the couple soon began to live with youthfulness for the second time in their lives. This time though Ravi took things lightly. He didn't strain himself with work and instead added pleasure to it by involving sightseeing, taking his wife along with him everywhere as she was now free from her motherly duties.

The Mumbai house began to be getting a lot of ventilation as they began to go there often for longer periods. The city was simply marvellous in its rush; the cinema halls, the huge malls, the shopping arcades were indeed mesmerising but deep down she always longed to return to Pune. Perhaps it was her roots that pulled her back to the simple lifestyle of her home town. Pune too, she had noticed was becoming more commercial and more and more Mumbai like day by day and she silently wished that it wouldn't someday become a mini Mumbai.

Years passed by and they were blessed with two lovely grand-daughters who Ravi doted on. She noticed how he spoilt them with ice-creams and chocolates every time they visited them. The girls were little well behaved rag dolls. Their hair ran loose in curls all over their face as they ran in their grand-parent's house in their cotton floral print dresses. When Shusmita saw the little girls hug, kiss, punch and fight with one another, she realised how Prajakta as an only child must have felt while growing up. As a young girl growing into her beautiful youthful self, her darling daughter had often complained of loneliness. The little girls pulling at her sari brought her back to the present and she silently blessed her daughter and her family.

As the days passed by, Ravi expressed a desire that he had once again got tired of work that made him journey around constantly and instead expressed an urge to stay home as far as possible. However he was tensed about how he would manage with a reducing income. Besides his earlier investments, there had to be something more which could be like the constant flow of river water continuously supplying a fresh stock to an otherwise depleting monetary condition. He wanted his family to continue to live in the same lavish manner that they had always managed to live in. After all, every time his daughter and grand-daughters came to visit them or spend a few days with them, the largeness of his heart never let them return without bags full of gifts.

"Sush, I think it's time we rent out our Mumbai flat. Mr. Suresh our neighbour over there just called me up a few days back suggesting this to me as we don't seem to be going there too often. He said that he knew of some families who would be interested if we were willing. What do you suggest? The rent there will be good and instead of keeping the place locked up, it would be certainly much better."

The decision was finally made. The Mumbai apartment was given out on rent. Living on rent was extremely stressful for those who rented the place, but for the owner it was like a lottery in that city. The city attracted all kinds of people, from all classes of the society. By now the property rates had as if touched the sky; making it virtually impossible for even well-to-do families to afford buying the stone structures there. Ravi had indeed been a wise man, and the decision he had made earlier investing in a place, was now at a stage to bear fruits.

A middleman was brought on the scene and the apartment was let out on rent. They had strictly decided to let it out only to families who came to the city for work or education of their children. The place was in an environment which had ample scope of generating wealth due to the availability of job opportunities and some of the best educational institutions situated very close to it.

Every time a new tenant approached them, either Ravi or Shusmita went to Mumbai to sign the terms and conditions documents. Several instructions had to be given verbally in spite of the written ones to put emphasis on them. 'No nails to be drilled in the walls', 'No extra decorative fittings', 'No changes to be made in the structure', and so on.

To their luck, Mumbai had by then become the most expensive city in India and the rent with every new client was always on an increase. The more the demand, the more the price, was a simple logic Shusmita had understood; and the system had toughened her and Ravi to put their emotions on hold when certain families wishing to extend their stay, pleaded for a reduction in the otherwise mounting rent. There were too many rich and happy fishes in the pond of life to bother about any sad or troubled ones or pay heed to their inconveniences. The rule had always been 'survival of the fittest' and they did not feel any guilt when a family vacated their apartment with anguish and concern after being refused an extension.

Everything seemed to be going on perfectly well when Ravi's health suddenly once again began to deteriorate. The doctors had no clue what so ever. All the required medical tests once again had no answers to his failing health, but it appeared as if his life's bank balance was certainly falling drastically. Whether in Pune or Mumbai, the doctors were emptying their savings with every visit they paid to them. With the man in the house getting weaker and weaker day by day, Shusmita's trips to Mumbai got interspersed with trips to different religious destinations, where she humbly went begging to all the Gods for her husband's good health and long life. Every time she returned with some prasad, Ravi smiled with some insight about himself which he appeared to be hiding from her. The dying man perhaps somehow knew that no matter what his wife did, she would not be able to hold him back for long. His contractual stay on the planet was coming to an end and no extensions were ever given here.

Holding his hand she comforted him, "You must not give up hope. We are doing all we can. We'll go to the best doctors and the best hospitals, but please for my sake hold on. You will get well. There is nothing wrong with you. You must persist. The Gods can't be deaf to our pleas. Don't give up the will to live. The Gods will surely listen to our heart's desires........." her words were cut short when the telephone rang. "Hello", their Mumbai occupant was on the line. "Madam, I know that our contract ends on the 15th of this month after which we had planned to leave and go back to our hometown Morbi, but…." she cut him short. "I'm sorry Mr. Patel, I have already signed a contract with the next client and they are arriving in Mumbai on the 16th. I will not be in a position to help you out." The voice at the other end became heavy, "Madam please be kind and understand my problem. There are very few colleges back home and we came here only for the sake of our child's education. But to our bad luck, one exam has got postponed due to the teacher's strike at the Mumbai University and now it's to be held on the 20th of this month. It's just a matter of 4 more days and I promise that we'll leave immediately the next day after the exam. Where will we find a place in this city for just 4 days madam? My son Suraj will also get disturbed in his study pattern and this examination is very important for his future. This exam means a lot to him madam. It's just a matter of 4 days, please do try and make some adjustments." She had often heard such pleas, but experience had made her emotionally thickened with them. How could she keep looking into the personal problems of her clients? She had to take care of her family first. After all entries and exits were, a rule of life. How would life continue if she kept giving the tenants extensions like this? When it was time to pack up, it was time to pack up. A few drops of tears couldn't disturb the ocean of life whose waves rose and fell with the tides of time. She was sitting with the mobile in her lap and thinking about which other hospital would have better doctors to diagnose Ravi's problem. She had to find a way to help her husband get better. There had to be someone somewhere, who would have a remedy for his failing health. She would never stop trying.

The phone was ringing again. It would be that Patel again. She cursed him in her mind "That fellow is quite a persistent chap," she thought, and wondered how she would deal with him if he refused to leave. She had no time to leave Ravi's side and go to Mumbai. Her thoughts once again went to Ravi's health. Suddenly Ravi began coughing violently breaking her chain of thoughts. She quickly got up and ran to the kitchen to fetch him a glass of water, but when she stood beside him and put the glass to his lips, Ravi had moved on. She was too stunned for any reaction. As water trickled down the sides of his lips, she stood fixated looking into her husband's face. Her lips curved gently, the Gods too were very busy with their other jobs and perhaps couldn't give her husband an extension. She bent down on her knees in submission to the Almighties will and touched Ravi's face with nervous hands and smiled with tears in her eyes, "Yes Ravi, the contract has expired."

FREEDOM FROM TURMOIL

It was a firm 'NO'. It was quite loud, clear and emphatic; though it was nothing really new for Paulomi. The last few years had passed by listening to refusals for the sake of her good.

"We can't take a risk. It is no longer safe for you to move all alone."

They loved her too much to let her get hurt anymore and also land themselves in any further trouble as caretakers. After all it was not only the patient who suffered, but to a great extent it was also the performers of care who had to go through a rough time especially if they had an emotional bond with the patient. Their days went by in her service and their nights in prayers for something miraculous and good to happen to her. It was almost as if worry had snatched away sleep from their eyes. They hadn't been the same before the accident. They were a people always open to exciting outings and adventurous events. They characteristically were personalities who heartily enjoyed life, taking great relish in every nuance of it. Of course it was the circumstantial happening that had to be held responsible for their change in behaviour which after all was very likely to happen to anyone whose child was hurt.

Parents loved their children beyond what any words could explain and her case was no different. When she insisted to get back the old ways of living, her mother resisted forcefully.

"Yes, I agree we were all so very different in our approach before, but don't forget that the accident hadn't happened then. That horrible day changed everything in our lives."

She had at times seen her mother wipe away a tear, not aware that she had been watched in her weakness. Her accident had succeeded in transforming the fearless spirit of her parent's open mindedness to that of a fearful flock of sheep who were always timid and hasty to seek shelter under camouflaging and protective foliage in the forest of mean and nasty wolves. How could she blame them for what they had become today? She wasn't ungrateful but instead in the silence of her heart she incessantly thanked them for what they had been in the past and also for what they were now. The fact was that they had been shaken up, and didn't want to face any more risks. What had to be, they had borne with as much courage as they could have gathered in their bodies, minds and hearts; but they were as if drained off of all physical, mental and emotional strength. 'No more', 'Not again', was the terminology she got to hear every day.

She felt sorry for them and the sufferings that her accident had caused them. Their suffering was of course not imaginary. She had seen their hearts bleed. Though she had been the victim, they had suffered the pangs of emotional pain much more than her physical one due to their love and responsibility towards her. "That's because we love you", they said. She understood their worries, but why didn't they understand her need to slide away the emotional curtain they had drawn over her to protect her from any more harmful rays of life?

"Dad, mum, I feel suffocated. I want my freedom again. I hate to live like this; always protected."

Life had put her into a boxing ring where even ordinary tasks had become very difficult for her to manage independently. However, then this was a conflict she knew she would have to face alone; and seeing their faces always heavy with thoughts and worries, didn't make it easy for her.

At her age there was so much to explore; the wadapav walla at the corner of the street, the panipuri vendor who sold delicious plates of puris with spicy water at the railway station, a latest film which had just been released in a suburban theatre, were all the things she kept missing. It was as if her legs had locked up her life and told her that there could be no more explorations in it. She had the courage which they could never imagine; but how could she convince their fear? Their love had as if put her into an exile which sometimes made her bitter seeing the same surroundings day in and day out. At such times her empty mind began to feed on doubts. Was it the truth that they kept her sheltered because they loved her immensely as they said they did, or was it that they were too scared and over tired of the burden that she had become now, and that then was in truth what kept them sheltering her to safe guard their future troubles? After all, their shoulders which were no more as strong as those of the youth had borne enough of her weight. It appeared to her that any more of the load of her responsibility would break their niceness if she persisted with her desires to explore the world around her like normal people did.

The world, they often explained to her was a very uncaring place. They were concerned and had time and again warned her reminding her that she certainly couldn't expect the world to be as caring as they were towards her. "The entire world is not your family which will time and again wish you good and take care of you or worry about your good health and happiness. Its time you understand your handicap and live life according to it." Her brother was quite vocal with his thoughts unlike her parents. Perhaps he was angry with her and the accident that had changed all their lives. He was young and wanted to be a free bird, but her parents kept reminding him of his responsibilities, insisting that he had duties to perform for his sister. She felt sad for him and never objected to the angry remarks he passed at her in his frustration.

The world didn't matter to her; though its uncaring hurry did let life pass by her like the lash of a wind which gave a rough edge to existence, but actually that was not what bothered her. What she needed was the support of her loved ones to help her learn to sharpen her emotional and physical handicap and reshape it beautifully with an artistic picture of strength.

"For how long will I remain a burden on you people? Please allow me to live my life on my terms. I certainly appreciate all your care and concern, but I feel imprisoned with such fearful emotions of care and worry."

She could never forget the day her father had brought her a ladies bike. The joy on her face which had been captured by the camera, she sometimes leafed through in the photo albums. Always wanting speed in her life, the public transport was too long a wait for her dashing personality.

In fact at times the long winding serpentine queues at the bus stands and rickshaw stands created for her a hindrance in the way of her speedy success. Her parents had given in to their darling daughter's request and gifted her to their dismay, her dream of speed.

Then the joyful race had begun. It had never been more fun to go from home to college and back home. It had never been so exciting to visit the bania with an empty bag to get it filled with the groceries. It had never been that adventurous to go to the theatre with expectations of wild imaginations and to return home with sometimes a satisfied mind and at times anger at the disappointment at the roughness of the character sketches which could have been more sharpened.

It was all going just too good to be true until the ill-fated day, when though she had stuck to the rules of the traffic; a taxi driver not paying heed to those same rules had come dashing towards her, breaking the signal and crushing her legs up in a collision. Life had suddenly woken her up in a hospital bed with no sensation in her legs. Her dashing spirit had been dashed in the road crash, hampering her down to almost never get up again. No more was there the spritely walk, though the wheel chair had been kind enough to allow her movement not restricting her to one place at the mercy of someone to come and help her.

The city still had not learnt to be wheel chair friendly. This made her sad time and again, as such an unfriendly environment for the physically disabled caused a lot of inconvenience and emotional disturbances to them. It had now been three years since that accident and since then she had been pleading for freedom to live on her own terms like she had earlier. But her accident had jolted her parents and they had fear pasted on their hearts to give ear to her requests. After all she was their precious daughter and they had almost missed losing out on her once; how could they even think of taking a risk again. Though it had only been her legs which after that torturous day had lost their movement, her life had as if lost its breath and instead gone static in enclosed captivity.

"Mum, if it had to happen, it happened, but now I can't live indoors for the rest of my life. You need to understand my need for independence and allow me movement on my own. I know you are there with me everywhere but that's what I don't want. I don't want my disability to be screamed out to the world. Please let me be on my own like before. After all I am not the only disabled person in the world."

"But you are not the same as you were before. The changing times need our approach towards life to change too. And it's not that we have locked you up; you do go to college don't you and we do take you for short outings too, don't we?"

"That's exactly what I'm trying to tell you. Times have changed and I've accepted the change. I am thankful to you that you at least allow me to go to college, but I miss those old times when I went everywhere else too. The accident has changed me from the outside; but that me inside the outer me, is still the same; I am no different on the inside even today but you seem to miss seeing that." Her father had just entered the room but before he could say anything to stop her expressing herself from demanding her freedom, she continued, stopping him with a hand raised up indicating that she needed to talk. "Please mum, please dad, please give me a chance to live my life. I beg you to try once again to trust me with myself. What happened in my life was not my fault; please don't punish me for it."

"It's just that your father and I wish to be more careful about you. If you misunderstand our care and love to be a punishment then we are sorry, but we can't help but protect you. And if something again were to happen to you, how would we manage? At our age this much has been enough."

Three years had passed by and yet her pleading for freedom had not borne any results. Her need for independence had fallen on deaf ears. She had been a blooming bird when life had cut off her strength to stand, as if plucking her out of it, like a growing fragrant flower had been pulled out of the life giving mud. Now she was instead a flower living a plastic existence in a vase kept safely in a corner where though it could be seen by all, it was better kept away for the safety of its frailty.

The word 'feminine' had in it the implications of beauty, delicacy and attraction, but feminity according to her was not just about being beautiful, delicate or attractive. It was about reaching out in all independence to accept ugliness and mould it to a new kind of beauty which the eye alone would fail to see. It was about the delicacy of emotions to hold them in all gentleness and care without crushing them with fear. It was about being attracted and allowing attraction with a free choice and respect of one's independent decisions.

Feminity in the usual sense as understood by a majority of people was in fact a big hurdle for those who believed the world needed domination and allowed it to be dominated by the fiercely strong. The male sex had been gifted with a physical power which could be used rightly to protect the physically weaker female sex and she at times wished that she were a man not because she loved wearing pants but simply to escape overprotectiveness.

But today her friend Sanjeevani had succeeded in doing what she hadn't in the last so many years been able to. Sanjeevani was her best friend she had grown up with in her neighbourhood. It was with this friend that she always had shared all her joys and worries, but now the dear friend was getting married, and would soon move away to another place. She knew that she would never be able to replace a friend like that. The loss of her freedom due to the accident and now the loss of a close friend were enough reasons to make her feel downhearted. But Sanjeeevani had included Paulomi in her wedding plans and had warned or rather threatened the crippled girl's already dismayed and distressed parents that if her friend was not allowed to be the bridesmaid, she wouldn't hesitate in calling off the wedding.

"Aunty, I promise you that if you do not allow Paulomi to be my bridesmaid, I will call off my marriage even at the last moment." Sanjeevani had spoken to her parents when she had come in to give the invitation card for her wedding.

Such stubborn behaviour had managed to open the doors of protection and security which had been bolted with an enormous lock of fear on the door of her parent's heart. A small opening had forcefully been made, and the fresh breeze of freedom had moved in finally to touch Paulomi's longings of escape.

Finally when the day of the wedding did arrive, the crowd was seated eager to get a glimpse of the bride in her beautiful red sari with lots of golden bangles on her delicate wrists and her face shining with wonder at what her future held for her. Paulomi was equally excited; she too was today going to be allowed to step out into an uncertain future all by herself. Her friends were all beautifully dressed; some in the traditional dresses and some in the lately accepted and modern styles, and amidst all that movement of happiness she rolled herself into the atmosphere of joy, pushing the wheels of the wheelchair with her hesitant but independent hands.

As she entered the gathering, her friend Sanjeevani took great pride in what she had succeeded in achieving. She turned to look at her and smiled, getting in return a thank you which only her ears could hear.

As she rolled herself towards the bride, Paulomi looked beautiful in the long white skirt and a lacy pleated white blouse. With a sweet and quiet smile she acknowledged her saviour showing appreciation for rescuing her from the clutches of protective concern and bestowing her with the freedom of uncertain independence.

FEAR

Poornima was lucky. She had been born in a Hindu family which had left its shackles of orthodoxy far behind to its ancestral days. Right from her childhood when she had begun to think for herself, she had been encouraged to approach everything with a questioning mind. Everything in the world of her dwelling, all those experiences were open to inquiry; and such an interrogative approach had helped unravel matters which otherwise normally left a large number of people bewildered. She knew well that life could never be the same for all and she had learnt to receive dissimilarities without an opinionated mind. Diversity in life was natural after all.

She was glad that her family upbringing, education and life in general had taught her not to be judgemental and inflexible. She had been educated to believe in the oneness of the world and the singularity of the object of worship in spite of its different appearances. She remembered very vividly the day her son had arrived home to communicate to her his love for an American girl. She had then not felt even a little bit unhinged as she had smiled on hearing his announcement expressed with a little bit of hesitation in his voice. With an open mind she had accepted his choice and spread her arms wide enough to embrace her son and his preference in life.

Her daughter-in-law was a wonderful young lady and in spite of her light skin colour and a contrary shade of hair colour to the rich lustrous dark mane of the Indian woman, she was equally beautiful.

Years had passed by and in that time period she had visited the foreign land many a times taking with her bags full of Indian colours as gifts to adorn the pale skin of her daughter from another land and every time she had felt that she looked even more beautiful than before.

****

Poornima's once upon a time raven black head now looked like the snowy peaks of the Himalayas. As she sat lazing on an easy chair, letting her old bones soak in some sunlight to enhance the vitamin D to absorb the calcium form her diet, she gently ran a large toothed comb through the waves of her hair. Her eyes looked vacantly into the peace surrounding her in the atmosphere, when suddenly her body jerked into painful memory. The pleasant atmosphere of the present times had not always been so. Her ears even today, very clearly, could still hear the shrieks of pain which had passed through the air in spite of no transmitter of sound. The shrieks were the soul cries of pain her people had experienced. Touching her hair gently she smiled to herself remembering how perhaps each strand on her chalky head could speak a story of the torments her eyes had witnessed. Her relaxed muscles as if suddenly experiencing pain, tensed up to harden her heart and make it strong to face the agony of the past. A cold summer wind suddenly blew on her face to ease her and she got up leaving the reclining chair to walk back into her house and take a much needed short nap at her age.

****

It was a warm day. The sun shined brightly to balm all hearts. She liked the heat of the sun as it kept the cold memories of her past away from her. As the phone rang like every day, she knew it would be Gaurav calling up religiously in his usual caring manner. It was even more of a pleasure when Ann called up. The way she pronounced 'mama' was like the soothing effect of a cold pack to a sprained limb. Today however, Amar had some news for her. Lalita, her granddaughter had found a man for herself. Yusuf was a qualified engineer whose ancestors were from Pakistan.

Poornima didn't sleep that night. As she tossed and turned on the bed fighting with sleep which refused to come to kiss her closed eyelids she realised that she had changed. Her reasoning capacity no more evaluated the merit of a person on the basis of his intellect and his personal life, but instead on the caste he belonged to. The abundance of acceptance which she had had earlier, suddenly seemed to have reduced and her mind felt itself closing in on certain thoughts. Her son had earlier in one of his regular mails texted her about his daughter's wedding plans but then she had no idea who the young man in her grand child's life was to be. Now after knowing about the man to be entering her family circle, she was much upset to learn that Lalita, her grand-daughter had plans of shifting to Pakistan after her marriage and perhaps if she felt comfortable in her new home she would settle down for ever in that new place.

After a night full of disturbed sleep, she had the very next morning written about her concerns to her son.

"My dear Gaurav,

I am more than glad that my darling little Lalita has grown so big now that I will hear the wedding bells once again in this family. I still remember her as that little bundle of joy with light brown eyes and curly black hair running round the house every time you visited me here in India. Does she still maintain those curls or has she like the others, gone and straightened them out? I am really surprised how you who have always been a very possessive father have allowed her to make such a rash decision to stay far away from you. After all she is a girl, and in our Indian culture girls are very precious. They are the Goddess Laxmi from whom no one would ever want to part. They are the true wealth a family boasts off. To be very honest, I am not at all happy with this choice she has made and the one you very readily seem to have consented to. I don't say that Yusuf is a wrong man; but Pakistan? How can she go and live over there? My son, the child is young, but you are a matured man. Having left the Indian soil now for quite a few years, perhaps you have lost track of our past history. I know that I must not make a nuisance of myself by interfering in your decisions, but I am really worried. I have gone through the worst that you have only heard of, and never actually seen or born it on yourself; and I thank God for that. However before making any final decisions please do think again, not just once but many times.

May God bless you all,
Ma."

Since the day she had sent that email to her son in America, she had not slept well. Her past which had since long ago been well wrapped up in the coffin of time, had as if suddenly risen once again like a ghastly ghost to scare her. Unable to sleep, she often tossed and turned seeing amputated limbs and blood everywhere. She woke up screaming when she saw headless bodies beating their chests and walking towards her. Often in the middle of the night she sat up nervously on the bed, her body wet with the sweat of fright and her head throbbing with the pain of those alarmingly scary memories.

She had then been only about twenty and newly married when in the dark of the night Gaurav's father had worn three shirts, three pants and two coats and feeling too over stuffed, had begun helping her to tie a cotton bag packed with money and gold on her waist around which she had worn six saris, as what they wore was what they got to take with themselves. It had taken a great effort and expertise to look as natural as possible. She had had to be careful and look naturally pregnant.

All that had taken place so long ago and yet, every moment of that time had as if got imprinted on her mind; every minute of that traumatic period was so freshly available to her especially now when her grand-child had grown so big to talk marriage and senseless enough to plan it with a Pakistani man. The fears of her past had suddenly surfaced threatening the happiness of her future. She was indeed eager to see her great grand-children, but now fear encircled her heart. All that belief in one God and all humans being His children was all right but when the memory of her past got awakened, she hated…..

The blood her eyes had seen sixty five years ago had as if distorted her vision. It was not that she wished to hate any religion, but her heart had clasped the roots of insecurity too tight to detach from them even with the pull of time. And there was an inexplicable flowering of the plant of doubt in her psyche. No matter how sensible and rational she tried to be, the plant stayed young and refused to wither away with age. In fact every time she read or heard of a terror attack, the plant as if regained its youth and began to grow with an added zest. She longed to uproot this feeling of mistrust; she tried to exercise her old brains to remember the good that had happened before she had had to part with all that had belonged to them in a country which had suddenly one day woken up from what seemed to be a dream of unitedness and said that Hindus didn't belong to it.

Her mind flashed back to the school she had been to. It was like a stream of consciousness where she could see a group of older boys she passed by on her way back home from school. Her ears yet felt insulted when she re-caught those words. They echoed even today inside her ears: "She is a Hindu. We can pick on her." As soon as she had heard those words, her heart had begun to pace like a rabbit and her feet had caught speed. When she had finally reached home, her Muslim maid had hugged her tight and in that embrace, her speeding heart had found rest. At that moment she had not been less scared, but in those arms she had somehow hoped that no one would harm her; at least not in their presence and yet they had to run out to save their bodies as their spirits of brotherhood had got crushed.

As she sat alone today, with white hair having covered all of her head, she wondered if her grand-child would ever understand her fears. She wanted that little girl, now grown into a beautiful young lady, to prosper in her married life and live in a safe place. She wondered if that place where she had grown up, could be safe after all that she had gone through over there? Could the youth of today understand the troubles her generation had faced? Could they understand the fears the minds and hearts of the people then had experienced? That child was too precious to her, like all those children who had been precious to their near and dear ones; but who hadn't been lucky enough to escape that ghastly hatred. The world of the young was so raw and inexperienced to reality, how could she convince the child that life could change in a drop of an eyelid and that it would never be the same again?

She sat anxiously entwining her fingers in a nervous dance. What could she do? She didn't want the world to continue living in the memories of hatred, and yet the remembrance of bloodshed was not easy to be washed away with the ideologies of modernity and great speeches about brotherhood of mankind. Sometimes, life drifted one on the river of experiences in boats of relationships with oars of joy and sorrow and all one needed to do was row the boat with the strength of hope and glide over the waves of insecurity to safer shores of happiness, leaving behind the bleeding past. Perhaps the painful security of precautions at times needed to be left alone to experience the joys of the vacillations of the future.

I NEED TO TALK

With no access to a wash room, Parinita had got accustomed to use the water bowl in which she would otherwise clean the paint brushes. Thank God that she had two such bowls.

Never even in the wildest of her wildest imaginations had she ever thought that she would have to use an accessory of art for a purpose so filthy. She had decided that today when Rajendra would return from work in the evening, she would call it final. She was an educated woman and an artist in her own small way, though she had still not been able to collect enough money to hold an exhibition at the Cymroza art gallery at Breach Candy. She had held on to courage and persistence to continue with her dreams and never stopped painting in spite of the many hardships she had had to face on a regular basis due to her mentally disturbed mother-in-law. She had promised herself that under no condition would she ever put a stop to this colourful passion of hers; as it was these very colours which made her world bright even though most of the time she felt engulfed in darkness. They opposed the plain white or black sheets with their riot of matches and mismatches. In their bizarreness they added a harmony to her disharmonized mind.

She sincerely believed, that sooner or later, a day would surely come when her paintings would grace the walls of the prestigious gallery for people to see, and then, those with a keen eye and good taste would gather to appreciate the way in which she had managed to put her thoughts, all cuddled up inside her little brain, into different shapes, sizes and shades. She was sure that her paintings would someday soon sell like hot cakes; they would have to. Her paintings were her pictorial life story and hers was no birth, growth and death kind of an ordinary life.

****

It had been pouring outside the whole day. The incessant rains had brought the atmospheric temperature down drastically. Normally if it hadn't been that cold, she could have managed without urinating for the entire day, if only she would have abstained from drinking water; but it was not the same now. The weather had got quite chilled and after Sania's birth, she had somewhat lost control of her bladder. Left with no choice now, she had no options but to use the second bowl which she would keep aside for further use. The whole procedure besides being quite revolting was too uncomfortable. It wasn't easy to squat over a small bowl and aim at it taking care not to spill any of its contents outside on the floor; not even a drop of it. After the bowl was full, there was another acrobatic skill, which had to be completed when she had to lift it gently and overturn it outside the window to keep it empty and ready for another call of nature.

She could hear the key in the lock. Sania was probably hungry again. Her mother-in-law unlocked the door and gave her darling baby to her.

"Hurry up. I don't want your unpleasant touch on my son's child for even a second more than required." The old woman never left the room after she had given her the child, and instead sat right in front of her, spying on every emotion of hers. As she made herself comfortable on the bed, the old lady sat across on a sofa chair with eyes glued to her breasts as she unbuttoned her dress to allow Sania to fill up her little empty stomach with the milk of love overflowing from them. It was more than uncomfortable to see the woman's eyes taking in on the roundness of her flesh on which the tiny fingers of her child made a loving communication as they kept fondling her skin. Not being able to bear the embarrassment, she quickly pulled a shawl over herself to cover up.

"Put that down." The old woman yelled immediately. "I don't trust you a bit. The witch that you are, you have already poisoned my son's head enough. You better feed her in the open. What if you poison her too, what will I answer my son when he comes back home from work?"

The woman had gone crazy. Perhaps she needed help. Rajendra had told her about her past sufferings. Her husband had left her when she was with child and since then she had brought up her son single handed. Rajendra had shared with her, several sad and tough stories of hers; of how she had educated him in spite of herself being uneducated and many other such tales of her woe. With time, her single status and too many responsibilities had left her with certain traits, not accepted at large. She had developed obsessively possessive feelings towards her son. She was scared that he too would someday leave her like her husband had, and go away leaving her all alone. But who could inject her with a remedy of a much needed security?

"She is my child too. I have given birth to her. Why would I ever poison her? All mothers are not like you. Why do you do this to me? How can you? What kind of a mother are you?" She wondered if she had done the wrong thing by speaking like that to Rajendra's mother. She wondered if he would get upset with her when he returned in the evening. She was sure that when Rajendra arrived in the evening, the old woman would not spare her for the courage she had shown in her argument of the afternoon.

"Your child? My foot! You are just the ground in which a seed was planted by the farmer. You have no right to the crop that has grown on you. It all belongs to the farmer and what do you mean by saying that all mothers are not like me? I love my son and therefore am protecting him from a sorceress like you."

Pulling the reins of her anger she had tried to pacify the woman. She didn't know whether to get angrier or to sympathize with her. After all, her present condition was all the doing of the old woman. But why didn't Rajendra bring about a solution? Every night as she slept beside him, he convinced her to pull through it all for a little more time. "Just a few more days and she will be normal. I have spoken to a psychiatrist and he has promised a remedy for her behaviour. He is going to give me some pills to calm her. You will though have to be very careful, to not let her know about the medicine. You could mix it up in a glass of milk or tea that you give her in the mornings while she sits to have her breakfast with me before I leave for work."

She spoke pleadingly to the hardened woman, "What have I done to you or to your son to be called a witch? Why are you always so upset with me? Why can't you see us happy together? Why can't we all be happy together?"

Her mother-in-law did not answer her and instead simply puffed in her usual arrogance.

The baby had finished her feed and dozed off. Her face looked angelic with a little milk still spread on her pink lips. She looked at the innocently angelic face of her child. But before she could bend and kiss her on her forehead, the old woman pounced on her, literally scaring her.

"Give her back to me and don't look so deep into her with your evil eyes."

The door was locked again and she was all alone with her colours. The rains were a symbol of life to her. Every year with the first showers her brush began its work to fill the canvasses with stories of colours. Art was her life and the colours were the blood running through her veins. Painting was for her a dialogue with nature, where she spoke to the forces of the universe with the language of colours; she hoped that the finished paintings would speak to the hearts of the observers who would come to drink in the philosophy of the conversation she had had with creation.

This year though the rains had as if failed to inspire her; there was something different in the weather. The waters falling from the sky had escaped from giving her the usual refreshment of a creative flood and had instead brought with them a tsunami of tears.

The colours stood stuck up in the bottles. As she dipped the brushes into them, they as if refused to dance with a rhythmic movement. A picture too macabre was forming in her mind, but her hands trembled to sketch before she could give it any real place. She didn't want to drop the black of hopelessness, the orange of pain or the yellow of fear on the paper in front of her. Instead she wanted to shade the black background with the purity of the white, the silver of hope and the red of love. She hoped that all that was happening to her was a bad dream and that she would wake up with Raj's kiss on her cheek as a good morning alarm, and as she would move her hand by her side, she would feel her baby girl cuddling close to her breast.

****

It was 6.00 pm, the time when Rajendra normally returned home from work. She had decided that she would tell him how difficult it was getting of late, that she could take it all no more; that if he wasn't able to help her out with any solutions, she would pack her bags and leave tonight with her darling child to her brother's place.

But what would she tell her brother? She had always been taught not to wash her dirty linen in public. How could she disclose the dark side of her apparently sunny marriage to her kin? It would obviously disturb him. And then for how long would she pile on to him? He was no longer a bachelor, but a man with a wife and a family of his own to take care of. She didn't want to be a burden on anyone; not even her own brother. It wouldn't be right to invade his private world with her key of self-pity. But then, did she have any options? Probably there were no solutions in her life.

Some problems in life were like a road that led to infinity called hell. But she didn't want to travel to hell. She wanted to get off somewhere in between, to save herself. Hell had always been described as a place unbearable; where there was scorching heat and the pain of diseases and torture. It was torturous and sickening to pee in a bowl and then all the more disgusting to later lift it all up balancing it to throw out the contents from the window. She was a wise woman and she had to make the right choice of getting off the vehicle which was bent on journeying her to the abode of evil and condemned spirits. She could read her own mind getting disturbed in its depressive state and was worried that it had gained a depressive strength which could force her to throw herself out from the window along with the urine.

The key was once more moving in the lock. She hadn't noticed that it was 6 p.m. already; the time when Rajendra returned home. It was her time to be set free.

"Here you are." The old woman had opened the door. It was never locked up at Raj's arrival time. She wasn't as dumb and innocent as she acted in front of her son. Every time Parinita had told her husband that she was locked up in their bedroom soon after he left for work, he looked at her surprisingly as if to say that she was playing it a bit too harsh to blame his mother.

"It's now your time to move about free and entice my son with your evil charms and swollen body."

The bitch called her post-pregnancy weight a swelling. Her eyes were swollen with the desire of possession. She wanted her son to herself, but knew too well that if she held him back he would go mad like her and so she had planned his marriage as a public show of her motherly affection. She understood her as a woman wanting affection from her child, but what about the woman in her who needed to be rescued from the enticing ways of a wicked mother in law. Rajendra was full of pity for his mother and counted on her to be understanding and sympathetic towards the distress of the old woman, but he failed to understand the medley of her emotions which were growing dangerous for her sanity.

As she placed the cup of tea in front of her husband, she sat opposite him on the huge sofa. She felt so small in this place. It had succeeded in stripping her off her self-respect. However, gathering courage she spoke to him. But before she did that she made sure that her mother-in-law was not around to hear their conversation.

"Raj, I need to talk to you today. You can't brush it off anymore as insignificant. I am the one who suffers when you are out at work the whole day. Your mother is mad and you need to help her."

Rajendra was sipping on the steaming cup of tea she had served him. It appeared as if he was too tired and fed up of this issue she raised again and again. But she couldn't help it, as she was the one who was suffering every day after he left for work. He didn't seem to be much concerned with her troubles, or was it that he didn't believe that his mother could do that to her daughter-in-law the moment her son left for work. Collecting his strength and pushing behind his boredom he began to convince her as usual.

"After work yesterday, I dropped in at Guruji's. He said, 'anytime now'. She is of age. Please Rani let us forgive and let her move on with her journey. In these last days of hers, I don't want to create a scene with her. Even if all that you say is true, please for my sake and for the sake of our child bear with it. Only a few more days and then we will all be free. We will then replace these sorrowful days with tonnes of joy and forget the past. Help me help my conscience darling. I do not want to live for the rest of my life with a guilt that I left her alone when probably she needed me the most. After all…….please understand my feelings." He turned around to see if his mother was anywhere near them. Then he caressed her knee from under the table with his hand and continued, "She is my mother. She had to bring me up without a man in her life. She has worked too hard. It has not been easy for her. She is just over possessive about me and yes, of course I agree that it's not right to cause pain to another because of your troubles, but yet I beg of you to help me with your understanding by tolerating her for some more time."

She smiled at him and nodded her head as if to tell him that she would try her best but she couldn't understand how any person could foretell the time of the death of another. But of late, she had noticed that Raj had also been disturbed because of her constant complaints and had begun visiting a tantric baba.

The child's hunger had woken her up. She looked to see the time. It was 2.00 a.m., Raj was fast asleep peacefully. His mind and body had not been humiliated the previous day, nor did he have the fear of any progressive humiliation for the days to come. She could hear a whispering snore. In her mind she blessed him and wished a long and healthy life for him. After all, he would have to now take care of their child single handed.

The next day as Raj was returning from work, he saw a large crowd gathered outside the building. As he approached near, he saw that the crowd had collected exactly under the window of his apartment. As he went closer, his mother along with his neighbour came running towards him.

Wailing and falling as she tried to pull all of her weight in a hurry, the old woman looked quite scared and terrified. She was beating her chest in the fashion of moaning. "My son, destiny has been too cruel to you; how will you cross the journey of your life all alone now, and that too with the responsibility of a child? God has not been too kind to you my son. When I go up to Him, I will surely ask Him why He takes a silent pleasure in the sufferings of the innocents. Why is it that He cannot digest the happiness of His creation?

Raj stood there stunned hearing his mother's words. A tragedy had struck him and he knew the cause. His body suddenly became limp as if some power had sucked all force out from it. As he reached where Parinita lay on the ground with a pillow of blood under her head, his knees gave way. He slumped down near his wife's body and began to cry aloud.

"Why, why didn't you wait? It was not your turn to leave so early. Why didn't you wait as I had told you to?" He had never thought that she had truly been that troubled. If only he had known, he wouldn't have let this happen. He bent down close to the lifeless body and picked it up screaming in pain. He now understood that when it hurt, it hurt real bad.

INDEPENDENCE

Dhwani was nervous. She normally didn't take much time to get ready when she had to go out but today she was suffering from disordered nerves. She hadn't been able to decide whether a sari would be more appropriate or a dress, and then finally she had decided on the dress which she had chosen for herself when they had been to Paris many years ago and the one which Pranav had never liked on her.

She called for a cab to go to his office but when the cab did arrive she had a moment of doubt whether she was going to do the right thing or whether she should call it off and stay back at home. If she did that she knew that all the courage she had emotionally and mentally worked hard to build up, would all go to waste till another day when again another spurt of bravery would enable her once again to face life as it was.

At last she gave ear to her heart and got into the cab. She had no idea whatsoever how the silence of so many years had suddenly found an outburst to allow her thoughts to spill out into the vessel of her mouth, the contents of which she would today finally reveal to Pranav.

Her frame of mind for many years had been like a battle ground which had shaken up her sanity. The strange thing was that in this war of her conscience, the mind of the woman in her was being insulted by the subjugation of the heart of the neglected wife. The bold front that she had finally managed to wear today had taken her years to gather ammunitions of dauntlessness and a voice to express it. The initial murmurs of unhappiness had today found the need and pugnacity of vocalization.

She had this day, completed twenty years of living with Pranav. It was on this day of the calendar that they had got married. Over the years the calendars had changed and so had Pranav. Yes it was her wedding anniversary today and as usual Pranav hadn't remembered it.

Year after year she had planned celebrations for this day reminding Pranav of her presence and the need to acknowledge her. But today as she sat back to think about all the efforts that she had put into this relationship; she herself didn't know what she had been celebrating about. Perhaps it had been a tradition that she had followed. She had been taught to keep important days and dates in mind, as they mattered in everybody's lives and she had religiously done so. Birthdays, death anniversaries and marriage anniversaries were surely important days in individual calendars. Memories of those days in life were flooded with unfathomable emotions. Those important days opened the windows in the corners of her heart where she had safely locked up her joys and sorrows which she never would want to lose.

With changing times, people too changed and relationships went through modifications too, just as hers had with Pranav; but memories of those stupendous old days even today made her feel terrific about the wonderful times of the past in spite of the present not being that agreeable.

Normally the intelligence of man urged him to let go of his past and live for today, but in her case she had managed to keep herself happy with something totally different. According to her, she felt that if she were to let go of her past, she would have nothing to call upon her today. Her todays were intertwined with her yesterdays. But today she had realised that her marriage had lasted too long in its separate togetherness.

Though understandably living together, Pranav and she had developed separate views on everything under the sun. According to Pranav's understanding, every rule was made to be broken, whereas her heart and mind couldn't accept such dare devilry. Pranav laughed aloud at dirty jokes and she had got thankfully stuck to the simple ones which often set off the joys of kids running into contagious giggles. Pranav left food in his plate having finished his meal and she had been taught to respect every grain in the dish. Pranav kept cold water bottles on lovely polished furniture and she quickly kept a coaster under them to save the polish there. Pranav loved the noise of the television even if he wasn't viewing anything particular and she loved the quiet in the air with a book in her hand. Pranav never wore a seat belt while driving, throwing open challenges to death but she respected life which had gifted her with kids for whom she wanted to live and celebrate with them their joys in her old age. She had always wanted her children around her and he had always wanted her alone.

'But they are ours', she had expressed and he had said, 'Yes I know that, but they need not be in our bed room all the time'.

Today she wondered how she had managed to live with him all those twenty years. The children had grown up and were independent, but she had grown old faster than she would have wanted to. She wondered for how long she would have to continue living with him in her quiet sufferings. At times her silent anguish and discomfort in the relationship dipped her moral so low that she even contemplated death which at that moment she thought would certainly be better than a life alone in company with him. At times she reflected more with a feminist mind set and then she was contra distinctly a new person who couldn't wait to get him out of her life. His rudeness and snappiness were all so familiar to her today and yet she did hurt tremendously. There had been nights when she had prayed that he would be moved away from her and in the mornings she had been scared of her dreadful thoughts as without him everything around would become peacefully unfamiliar. It was this fear of the unknown that had made her continue to stick on to his nasty familiarity. But now it seemed that she had reached the rock bottom of her life and its artificiality was getting too unreal for her to cope with. She had lived twenty years in miserable security and now suddenly she had gathered courage to move ahead into a new joyously daring insecurity.

As she sat in the cab which was taking her towards Pranav's office, her mind began talking to her.

"So finally you have derived enough courage to oppose life?"

"You call it life? It has been hell for me and my children."

"You haven't seen real hell yet. A woman separated from her man is all alone in this big, bad world. It's a world where wolves prowl to catch hold of her."

"I have seen enough of a wild animal at home to be scared of the wolves outside."

"Actually what is it that is bothering you to take this drastic step? Have you consulted your children? They are now big enough to put in their suggestions."

"Yes they have grown up enough and therefore do not really need the constant care and concern of a parent. They have their own lives now. It's high time that I begin to live mine. If it won't be now then it will never be."

"But why, you certainly did manage for so many years, actually you did pull on didn't you?"

"Exactly, I did pull on but now I do not want to pull on any more. I want to relax. Look at me today, I look and feel so relaxed in this dress but he never appreciates it. He always expects me to wear saris. They are so cumbersome but he doesn't care for my discomfort. If he hates dresses on women then why doesn't he tell his secretary to stop wearing the short ones she wears to work daily?"

"You are a fool to crib about such silly little nothings. Life is too magnanimous to pay heed to such petty stuff. I didn't expect this from you. Over the years you have become a cribber even when there is nothing really genuine to crib about. Sari or a dress, how does it matter?"

"That's exactly what I keep telling him. How does it matter if I feel more comfortable in a dress? Why must he insist then on me wearing a sari only? But he feels that he owns me and that he can rule me in every little thing and he makes me obey him and change my likes and dislikes keeping his in mind. It's inhuman to treat someone in that manner for years and years. The sari and the dress thing is just one of the numerous ways in which I have been ruled for so many years. But now I am fed up. His outrageously meaningless and childish demands I have begun to find villainous and I want freedom."

"Go ahead then, and face life alone if you so insist." Yes, her assertively annoyed individuality which felt too burned out had to be saved from the collapsing of her self-worthiness.

"Surely I will. Even if you think I am a fool to do so; I will be a fool even if fools plunge into situations where wise men fear to tread. At least the fool will live in a fool's paradise. I am sure that it will be better than the wise man's hell."

"It will be a foolish short term joy which you will soon regret."

The cab had reached its destination and she had hardly noticed the long distance drive or the traffic which any other day would have added to her panic. Her self-analytical communication had saved her the trauma of the congested drive. She paid the driver his dues and unclasped the seat belt of security and moved out to face the new pathway of uncertainty.

As she walked towards Pranav's office she wondered if he too had been as miserable with her as she had been with him. Perhaps they both had hidden their feelings from one another. She suddenly noticed that her shoulders were drooping as she walked with a slow gait. She quickly straightened herself and put sprite into her walk. She knew for sure that if she kept thinking about the past again and again fearing the future, she would never get the freedom she so much was now longing for.

She knew that when she would give up this man in her life, she would be free of all the emotional trouble he gave her from day to day living with him, but she also knew that she would be giving up the comforts of the lovely home he had given her. She would be giving up all the plants she had nurtured over there as her children, tending to them as her own flesh and blood, touching them, feeding them with water and soil, playing soft music to them and burning incense sticks around them and then sitting in that cane rocking chair and pleasantly moving in a trance like motion to the silent music they played for her. Here too, many a times he had barged in suddenly in his characteristic harshness demanding his clothes and underclothes. She was fed up of choosing the right combinations of his trousers and shirts and the tie which he often knotted wrongly in his hurry. He was always in a hurry and she had in her silent aloneness just allowed him to pass by her.

As she entered the office, she felt everything strangely new. She didn't even remember the last time she had come here. Her own husband's place of work! She once again began to feel uneasy. Would she be able to do it today? There wasn't a look of surprise on his face as he saw her enter the office. She hadn't succeeded to take him unawares even for this once. As she walked close towards his table she realised his unaffected self; as if he had known that she was coming. But she hadn't told him. She hadn't told anyone. Not even her-self. It had been a sudden decision in just a moment of emotion which had perhaps came to a boiling point all of a sudden. Her eyes went to the bookshelf on his right amidst the books that he often used for reference. There amidst them lay a vase she had chosen for him long ago. She didn't now remember from where exactly she had picked it up. Perhaps she had bought it from one of those exhibitions that they had visited during the Dusshera festival. She noticed the dust on her gift and realised that it had been left unmoved or untouched since long. The reference books near it hadn't collected the dust but it certainly had as it lay in a corner like she did in his life; sitting just there, colourful and beautiful but not making any difference. He hadn't told her to sit down. Perhaps she was so much a part of him. After all you wouldn't tell yourself to sit or keep standing. You let yourself free to do as you pleased and perhaps he was just doing that. But it could also be that he didn't care and she was being ignored. The debate had once again begun in her mind. She wished she hadn't come here. How could she just stand there and announce that she wanted all the past, all their past, to be wiped out. If her life were a slate, she could have wiped it clean; but this was a great span of throbbing energy. How could she wipe away the emotions, the pains and the pleasures, the joys and the sorrows from this vibrant period? They were all so intertwined, the past and the present. If she dared to cut a part out, how would she survive with only the other half? Worries once again chained her mind which was screaming for release. What was it that she was worried about, was it the future days which would become lonely or the nights which she would have to spend all by herself; alone? But hadn't she always been alone? Now perhaps in her single new status that she was going to ask for, she could give herself the alone time to fill up with hobbies of her likes; unlike the past crowds of his socialising where even in the midst of his colleagues she had often sat lonely.

She tried pulling out a hanky from her hand bag to wipe the beads of perspiration that had formed around her upper lip due to nervousness. She pulled the chair to sit on it not realising that there were wheels under it and in her jittery state of mind, missed sitting on the seat as the chair suddenly moved away dropping her with a thud to the ground.

Surprisingly, she was not embarrassed. She began to laugh aloud at her silly self. How just like that chair, her youth had slipped past her, robbing her of her seat of happiness; happiness which should have filled her instead with exquisite brightness to see with an elegant eye the artistry of life. Instead, she had been engulfed in the darkness of duties. The 'shoulds' and the 'musts' hadn't given her the opportunity to let in the 'ifs' or the 'maybes' to penetrate the rigidity of his kind of living, giving it the zing and the excitement to feel the rush of blood during the curves of a joyful acquaintance.

Pranav jumped out of his chair. "Are you hurt? How silly could you be? You could have injured yourself. Come let me help you", he extended his hand to pull her up. But in her giggling mood she refused his help. Slowly she managed to pull herself up independently.

"Really Pranav, I have indeed been very silly. I have hurt myself enough for so many years living with you and your silly attitudes towards life. I have in fear of being alone, allowed injury to my emotions and my soul, which has felt so cramped with you. But now I don't want my life to slip by like this chair any more. I'm going to hold it tight and live it the way I desire. Actually after so many years of living your desires, I have almost lost track of mine. But I'm going to search for them; I'm going to dig them out of the deep recesses of my heart. And I'm going to laugh at my stupidity to have suffered you for so many years. Pranav I want to write the story of my life from now on, and I have realized that I can't let you hold the pen any more. I want a separation from you. Perhaps you too will get happiness as the showers of my joy will fall on everything around me."

Pranav stood stunned. He simply kept looking at his wife.

KADAR (CARE)

It was Ankita's birthday today and everyone was in a joyful mood. A lot of planning and preparations had been put in since the last few days. Balloons, cakes, pastries, cookies had been arranged at the table for a quick grab of delight. Kadar was a small place; an island in itself which overlooked a slum area where hygiene seemed to have flown away on the wings of a bird leaving behind dirt of basic insufficiencies.

"Oh! You shouldn't be doing all this for me", Ankita mumbled with all her shyness enveloping the attention that she was receiving today. Suniti and Jeevan instantly were close by her side.

"But we want to do it. We feel good. Don't you like celebrations? It's nothing big you know, just a small gesture of happiness; and the others will enjoy too. What else do we humans have in our lives but the joy of gathering contentment and blessedness? Beautiful days like this one, are the times we need to cherish and not skip in the hurry of living. Sunil chacha, Rohini Tai, Prafulla devi and our beloved Amit kaka have also been looking forward to this special day. We aren't many over here at 'Kadar' you know, and so we need to make the best of the few birthdays we have to us."

Both the youngsters took Ankita's soft hands in theirs and rubbed her white skin with their fingers. Jeevan continued, "Don't you worry about anything. It makes us feel good to see you smile. All you have to do is to simply enjoy and keep being happy."

A little smile began emerging on Ankita's face. "Thank you so much. How will I ever repay you two for all you have been doing for me? Did you call him and tell him about today?"

Suniti came to Jeevan's rescue. "We were not able to get through. The telephone line seems to be having some problem. But don't you worry. As soon as the lines are cleared, we'll let him know". To get her more involved in what they were doing, she continued, "Look here, we have got a camera too. We'll mail him your beautiful pictures. He's sure to feel the pinch of missing such a beautiful occasion of indulgence in his life time. A mother's birthday is a time of great festivity for a child. We're sure you must have celebrated all his birthdays as he was growing up. Birthdays are a jubilation of life. Life is a great gift Kaki, a gift to be glad about."

Ankita took a deep sigh and turned her face away from the young couple who managed this place wonderfully sharing a lot of care and love with the few residents there. She knew how fortunate she was to be looked after and she also knew that not everyone was as fortunate as her to witness such a manifestation of love and yet she wished such care had come to her from her own child. Today she had entered the last decade of a century of living. She wished her son had taken out some time for her; at least this one day. But the world moved on. Like a small child she began sobbing. "Every need of his, every moment of my life, I spent looking after him and today where is he when I need him?"

These two children at the organisation did so much for her. How was she related to them? She wished they were her own. It had been a long twenty years since she had got herself admitted at 'Kadar'. 'Kadar' was then a small nursing home in the suburbs of the city and it was gradually becoming big with the need of the society, expanding itself into a care centre which extended with the magnanimity of the heart of its initiators, a support to those who due to their growing age couldn't support themselves. Palliative care was comparatively a new concept in India and she was one of the few lucky ones to have received it. Gaping into thin air she wondered whether she could really call herself lucky in spite of not being taken care of by her own child and getting support from strangers for the payment she had sensibly arranged for.

Suddenly Suniti broke her trance. Taking Ankita's hand in hers she encouraged her to bring a smile to her pensive face.

"I'm going to do a manicure for you today, but before that I want you to take these pills." She opened a bottle of a rescue medicine which would sooth her stress levels caused due to depression, which she often suffered from. "Here, take these like a good girl. Look, I have brought this colour for your nails. Do you like it? It will suit your skin colour. Don't you think so?" She could see a vacant look in the eyes of the old woman as she held up the nail polish bottle for her to see.

Ankita looked down at her hands. They had been so different and strong then. How tiny and insecure Anil had been when he was small and she was the one to take care of him with her strength. She remembered how she had, years and years and years ago held his little hand in hers and taught him to write the first alphabets on the black slate she had got for him. He had been overjoyed when she had handed it over to him with a small box of coloured chalks. It had become a prized possession of his which he carried everywhere he went, even to the garden in the evenings. There he would play around on the swings and the see-saw with the other tiny tots as she would either stand by to watch him closely, or sit for a while on the bench by the side. Her eyes never left his sight though. He was her precious baby and she was his precious mama. At least that's how he made her feel when he began to cry if his eyes could not locate her in the crowd of mothers in the garden. Her eyes became glassy again. She often forgot that he wasn't anymore that small baby of hers; in fact he was a big man holding an honourable position in a company he worked for out of India. After completing his education back home, he had decided to venture out for better prospects to foreign lands and left her assuring her of his return which had eventually never happened. Left with only his past and the money he regularly sent her, she had developed a habit of talking to his memories.

"You are a great man today, building highways and sea-links to connect people, but you have no time to connect to your mother." Suniti and Jeevan both turned to look at her simultaneously. She was once again having a single throated conversation with her absent son. It was not something new to them; in fact they had actually got used to such mumblings of the old lady; but what could they do? At least such one-sided conversations with her unavailable son kept her away from going into a silent depression.

Ankita's history papers showed her as a widow, with a son working overseas. They had tried to connect to him many a times and every time he had excused himself due to some urgent work till they had finally understood and deciphered his lack of interest for his aging mother. However they hadn't shared their understanding with Ankita, as they didn't want to add to her existing misery of physical isolation from her family which consisted of only her son.

Jeevan assured Ankita, "Kaki, your son is a big man now. He is very busy. But you don't have any reason to worry. We are never going to leave you alone till he comes back to take you along with him."

She had doubts if he would ever come before her last moments and even if he did, she wondered if he would ever recognise her. He had left India forty years back and forty years was a long time. She had changed so much since then. Forty years back she had been a strong and an independent woman of fifty. Her skin had not wrinkled, her hair had still retained its original colour, her teeth had sparkled from in between her lips every time she had laughed, and most important, her eyes had had hope in them. But now the scenario was totally different. Strength had been totally drained out from her body, to her embarrassment she had even lost the independence to manage her personal hygiene, her skin had more wrinkles on it than her head had hair of which the few strands left had gone all snowy white with time. The dentures lay by the side of her bed; she found them very unnecessary and cumbersome to wear all the time and so she made use of them only at meal times and her eyes carried most of the time an empty look; the windows of her eyelids had as if opened up to let the bird of hope fly away.

Suniti had finished painting Ankita's nails. "There! It's done. See how beautiful your nails look! Where are your spectacles now? Ah here! Let me make you wear them. That's fine. Now tell me, have I done a good job?" Ankita nodded a yes with a smile. "Okay then, you now let your nail colour dry till I finish some work and come back in a moment." She left in a hurry leaving Ankita to wonder how the young lady managed to run around the whole day without getting tired. "Ah yes", she thought to herself, "She has youth by her side." These kids here were doing a job tending to all the aged people in the home and her son Anil was completing his never ending assignments in a faraway land. She thanked her stars that these kids had taken her charge. She was on the agenda of their profession or where would she have been now? She had grown to know Suniti and Jeevan since the last many years. They were a young medical couple who took good care of her. Perhaps God made only a few like them nowadays.

Suniti soon came back into the room bringing along with her a small box tied with a fancy ribbon and began to untie it for Ankita since the old hands trembled every time she had to hold on to something. Alzheimer had weakened her grip. As she opened the box, Ankita's eyes glowed seeing a lovely chocolate cake in the shape of a heart waiting to be cut by her. Her friends, from their different respective rooms had by now gathered around her. After all this was like a new family of hers, made up of people whose families had no time or place for them. Tears rolled down from her eyes onto her soft white cheeks.

'Thank you. Thank you so much. I wish Anil was here to see all that you two do for me……." She suddenly stopped speaking as if once again the drift of her thoughts had punctured her speech. Her face looked as if it had lost the battle of life which had become too heavy for her to bear. There was a sudden silence all around the place. There was a sudden emptiness felt by everyone present. A balloon tied to her bed on this occasion of celebration suddenly let out all its air and hung limp. The cake waited to be cut as Suniti and Jeevan held Ankita's frail body. Perhaps she had no desire to cut the cake in her son's absence, they thought. Suniti held on to the side of the bed as if the old lady's exit had pulled at her life force too. After a few moments, the time everybody took to let the truth sink into them, Suniti gently took out the cell phone from her coat pocket and dialled Anil's number. There was a shocked silence in the room, but the voice at the other end was as usual in a hurry. "Yes tell me, how is my mother?"

"She has just moved on. We will wait till your arrive."

"Oh!" There was a moment's silence at the other end of the line. "It wouldn't make any sense now, would it? Coming all the way when she is no more. I have to thank you for all your help. Would you please complete the last rites and inform me about the expenses? I would be obliged."

Suniti felt speechless on hearing those words. Joy and grief had got too adjacent suddenly for her to gather grip of the either individually. But she knew she had to take charge of the situation. Jeevan laid his strong supporting hand on her shoulder and her mouth drew courage from that gesture of sharing strength to continue to speak.

"Thank you sir, we could manage that on our own. We may not be as rich as you in wealth, but we are neither as poor as you in heart. We just thought we needed to inform you. Good bye. Oh! By the way, just for your information, social services are an accepted intervention with their caring professionalised workforce in the land you have chosen to make your home. Just a piece of advice, do enrol yourself in advance for your lonely old age."

Disconnecting the line she put the cell phone back into her pocket and touched Ankita's head. With tears in her eyes she brought her lips close to the cold forehead. "Don't worry", she whispered, "we are there for you. You are not alone."

Turning to the side table where she kept the medicines, she helped herself to the bottle of the rescue drug, opening its lid she took a few pills for herself. Everybody needed to be rescued. Some from the loneliness they suffered in their lives, and some who understood the feelings of such loneliness.

Sunil Chacha, Rohini Tai, Prafulla Devi and Amit Kaka communicated a deeper understanding with one another. They had lived long enough to comprehend the tides of joys and sorrows. These grey and white heads had no tears in their eyes, their minds appeared devoid of thought or reflection, and yet their faces were a unified display of an understanding of life. Just a few minutes back, they had all placed themselves comfortably around Kaki's bed but now slowly they got up to move away to their respective rooms.

THE MOUNTAINS ARE SHEDDING TEARS

Shirin had to take the packed lunch to her brother who was at school. Her mother had kept it ready but when she was just about to step outdoors, the older woman screamed out loud.

''Where is your veil Shirin?'' She hated covering her head and face behind the cotton scarf. The cool breeze of Kashmir was so refreshing to the skin. It was like a mother's loving and amorousness towards her child. However she didn't want to argue with the elders at home. The men at home, her father, grandfather and her father's younger brother were given great respect by her mother. She knew that her grandfather who at that time was reclining on the rocking chair in the backyard, could hear every word of the argument she could pursue due to her irritation, and so she kept quite and silently turned back indoors to take her dupatta with which she stifled the voice of reason and instead covered her face right up to her lower eyelids without giving vent to her anger and instead with her head bent in frustration left the house to go to the school. As she was just about to shut the main door, she turned to look at her mother and her eyes spoke questioningly to her.

'Enough?' She gave a questioning glare at the worried woman.

'Will that do for now?

Her mother too turned her eyes away to some other work which perhaps needed more attention than the revolt of her young daughter. Also, she didn't want to strive and attend to any arguments with that immature girl.

Zulaikha didn't know for how long she would be able to hold tight that girl of hers, who day by day was spreading her wings to fly to newer destinations. The youth today, wanted freedom of mind, body and spirit and she wondered if they were wrong.

Kashmir was a beautiful place indeed. It was even rated as heaven on earth by many and yet it was not safe in that paradise like place for a young girl to move about without a veil. After all she was a mother, and she was worried about her child. Every time Shirin was out of the house, Zulaikha's mind as if went in a pause mode. She couldn't think of anything else. The food, the kitchen, even Abbu had to wait for his ginger tea till Shirin returned because Zulaikha sat on the rocking chair without rocking it, in a stiff silenced worry, till the girl returned home safely.

A new militant group had emerged in this beautiful heaven where their family had lived generation after generation, and it appeared to be hell bent on making this exquisitely radiant and naturally beautiful complexioned station of the creator look ugly. The Kashmiri girls had been warned to observe purdah and refrain from using mobile phones. They had been warned that if they didn't comply with the demand, they would be disfigured or even be put to death. Such groups surfaced time and again causing havoc in the lives of the civilians.

Shirin had just a few days back asked Zulaikha, why when there was so much beauty on earth were some people hell bent on destroying it? Zulaikha had explained to her growing daughter who was every day developing beautifully into a woman and whose mind too was longing for a great understanding of the world, which her greyish blue eyes were filtering in, that some people never allowed their minds to grow beyond the fortresses of their religions and therefore breathed the same stale air devoid of any freshness of knowledge. Their self-made religious borders therefore enclosed their lives into ponds of mucky waters which degenerated towards a thoughtless decomposing attitude like the green water in those ponds where no one with the need to wash himself would enter. Such a stinking hole of a well couldn't possibly give out a fountain of a life giving elixir.

"Alla is one my child; but different people call Him by different names. The saints come time and again to give this knowledge to the children of the Lord but some children have got schooled wrongly, which has conditioned their understanding; and their minds therefore no longer have the capacity to strip off their old beliefs and accept any new differences which could make life more lovable, agreeable and pleasurable."

"But how will women carrying mobile phones cause trouble to their religious zeal? The men are always allowed so many things, why are the women subjected to getting refused such basics of communication?"

"My child, the instrument opens up a new world of revelation which uncovers all that till now has been left concealed in suppression. It no more withholds any information. And an informed woman will certainly be a new woman who will be a threat to the world of dominating men."

"For how long amma, will we continue to be dominated? Your generation did not have the courage to rebel but I have the desire and the gut to do what my mind tells me is correct. At least allow me to go ahead and live freely."

Such conversations often took place between the mother and daughter when there was no one at home. Zulaikha understood the needs of the young girl, as she too had had the same hankering and thirst for freedom once upon a time; but which ultimately had been crushed under the dominance of her worrying father and possessive husband in succession. She hadn't forgotten the day when Fatima, their neighbour's daughter had been scarred for life. The girl had the same defying attitude of the youth that had been responsible for the new marked face she had got as a gift for her daring and bold resistance to the authority. Her youthful irresponsibility had made her venture out with impudence in spite of the handwritten posters which had threatened an acid attack on a face uncovered by a veil. She had no face now to step out with today. She was a lesson of fear the militant group had taught the others.

Shirin had delivered the tiffin box to her brother at the school, and now she was returning home to her worried mother. She knew that her mother's heart wouldn't rest till she was safe back indoors. Her feet moved as fast as she could move them to lessen the time of angst and worriment for her dear mother. She could see the snow peaked mountains from where the cool breeze played with her salwar making it flap around her covered legs, as if nature was happily playing with the material world, a part of which she belonged to. Of late though the snow was melting quite fast leaving the mountains considerably bare. She had heard of global warming but her heart had another explanation for the mountains revealing their brown skin from underneath their white jacket.

Since many years now, she had been noticing these tall mountains around her house. Their peaks reached close to heaven as if in a secret conversation with God. She wondered if these leviathan earth formations in their silence were having some celestial conversation with the blue yonder above and with their lofty understanding were astonishingly amazed at the turmoil and blood shed man could cause on a planet he was after all just visiting; and if they were simply sobbing at his forgetfulness.

THE OLD BRIDE

Kunti Chachi's joy knew no bounds. As soon as the news had reached her longing ears, she had rushed to the almanac to unearth her wedding sari which she had safely wrapped up in a muslin cloth to keep away from moths. Digging amidst the other clothes stacked up on top of the unused garment, one that had been lying untouched for almost six decades, she felt a sense of relief from the state of widowhood she had borne painstakingly for that long and arduous a period. Anxiously, she draped the soft nine yards around her stooping frame and patted the dishevelled white strands on her head to look a little presentable in the mirror.

Moving towards a corner table she opened the drawer to have a peek at an old photograph of hers which she had kept safely even after so many years. She remembered well the day it had been clicked; how clumsily she had fumbled then with the nine yards and posed to get permanently captured on paper with the sound of a click by a young photographer who had been specially invited for the wedding day.

Of course, at the age of eighty plus she did without doubt look strange dressed as a bride, but she couldn't have cared less. Nurtured with an undying hope; a string of which she had tied firmly to her heart, she was now convinced of her good-luck of getting back her husband who had finally found his way back home after having escaped from his marital duties when the kids certainly would have done better to have a father around them.

Bholanath had absconded from his wife, children and responsibilities without any pangs of guilt as if he didn't have a conscience; because the pathway of his life had not given him the happiness he had thought he deserved. The sole justification he had kept giving himself to ease any sense of responsibility in his heart so that he could escape from any remorse feelings, was that his marriage had been the decision of his parents and not his. He had wanted a different journey altogether; a travel plan where he would have freedom to explore the world at his pace. His appetite of joy had as if been restricted within the four walls and the two hugging and demanding arms of his new bride and his intense wish to journey at least a hundred miles away from his home had been crushed in a bear hug which was stifling and which had made him feel breathless. He had gradually then begun to feel displeased with the marriage that was restricting his heart's desire and so one fine day after fathering two children, when he couldn't any more bear the burden of their accountability whatsoever and the noise they made when he returned home from work every day in the evenings, he just left. One could very well have said that he fled or absconded or slipped or got away scot free from the responsibilities of living, but he couldn't have cared less and just moved out to the surprise of everybody who knew him, and never returned.

One fine day after having had his usual breakfast and reading the morning newspaper, he had very casually picked up the bag he carried every day to work and after the usual pat on Kunti Chachi's shoulder he had moved on. When he had failed to return at his usual time in the evening, Kunti Chachi had begun to wipe away from her forehead, beads of perspiration forming endlessly in spite of the cold weather. The days that followed, had been hell with two kids fighting for her one lap, and a missing husband, and to make it worse, no income to satisfy their hungry stomachs. Neighbours had then come forward with courage for her heart, hope for her mind and food for her plate. Time had moved on and things had of course changed. The kids had grown up and got settled in their own lives.

Today as she saw herself in the mirror, she smiled at her image which showed a very old woman bent with the weight of life she had been left to carry all alone on her frail shoulders. It had been a lot many years of living sans the company of a partner for a woman who once upon a time had nothing but love to give to her dear ones and a hope that they would return it to her. Those years hadn't just flown past. Every moment she remembered how she had lowered her dignity to live with the help of strangers to bring up her little children. She had not escaped humiliation as the world loved the language of taunts but she had borne it all with a humble attitude of expecting dignity in the future for her children. Engulfing herself in working and learning to survive single, she had at that time not realised a wound growing bigger in her heart. In spite of all the difficulties and vicissitudes of life, her children too had grown up good and got well placed in life. They had gradually moved out to live their lives, leaving her with occasional joys of celebrations where the family met for some moments to celebrate new happiness's or relive some pleasant memories of the old times gone by.

Of course she was no longer a young woman, but the old too longed for companionship. It was then suddenly one fine day that Bholanath had as if lost his way back home. He had been seen by a neighbour who had recognised him immediately and who had therefore rushed to Kunti Chachi to give her the news.

"Kunti ben, Kunti ben, I have brought you good news. Quickly put some sugar in my mouth."

Kunti Chachi's reflexes had with age become slow and she couldn't really understand why Yogesh bhai was making so much noise about some good news. Pulling herself up from the chair she had been occupying, she put aside the plate in her lap in which she had been cutting some vegetables for her lunch and walked slowly to the door where Yogesh bhai was standing.

"What has happened Yogesh bhai, what good news have you brought for me?" Yogesh bhai was panting after the speed his old legs had managed to pick up to reach Kunti Chachi's place.

"Bhabi, first give me something sweet to eat. It is no ordinary news I have brought." Kunti Chachi slowly turned to move towards the kitchen to get some sugar for the harbinger of excitement in her life.

"Here, take this spoon of sugar and now quickly tell me the good news. My old nerves can't bear the excitement for long."

"Bhabi, I saw bhaiya in the market."

Kunti Chachi would have collapsed if she had not held on to the chair beside her. "What are you saying? Are you sure? I knew, I knew it that he would come back for me. Why didn't you bring him back with you? Go fast my brother; bring him back before he vanishes again. This time I will not have the strength to bear separation."

The moment Yogesh bhai had turned to fetch her lost love; she had as quickly as her frail limbs could move rushed to the almanac to unearth her wedding sari. After so many years she was finally feeling wanted, and like a new bride began smiling to herself. After dressing up she walked to that small corner in her house which she had reserved for worship and where she had yet safely kept the small box of sindhur; the vermilion, which married women in India wore on their foreheads in honour of their marital status. With hands shaking with excitement and nervousness, she opened the lid and dipped her middle finger in the red colour and put it on her forehead between her eyebrows.

On hearing the good news her cheeks had as if suddenly got colour to them. As she turned to move to the door to wait for Yogesh bhai, she could see him returning with some old man. With her weak eyesight, she couldn't really see too well in spite of wearing her spectacles. She regretted not having made new ones as suggested to her by her sons. She had felt then that there was nothing worth seeing anymore in her life at her age. If only she had listened to her children, her joy today would have been doubled. But in any case after such a long period of separation unrecognisable changes were most likely to have taken place. The old man approaching towards her she could see, was carrying a stick and she moved to the side of the widely opened main door of her house to let him enter.

News soon reached her sons who were shocked at the audacity of their father and the simplicity of their mother. Doubt seeped into their minds. They needed a proof of identity and parenthood after so many years; they needed a reason for the re-join after so many long years of lacerating a pure loving heart; but how would they be able to explain such distrust and displeasure towards a man who had deprived them of their rightful inheritance of a parent to their mother? How could they express such feelings of emotional agitation to her, who they realised, was above all a woman waiting endlessly for companionship?

THE SECOND WIFE

For many men, a wife is indispensable. In fact for some men life without a wife would be unthinkable. For Santosh too, life had become anything but satisfactory. Every time he sat to heat a cup of milk for his children, he missed Shanti tremendously. He had never forgotten the day she had left home never to return. He remembered how he had waited till late evening that day wondering where she could have gone and why she hadn't returned; and when it was really late, he had finally gone to the police station to report her missing.

With two small children, an elder unmarried brother and an old father to take care of, Santosh wished Shanti hadn't just left like that. Actually she had not been a very pretty woman every man dreamt of for his wife, but she was a very hard working lady for whom her home and family were worship. In fact she had a deep gash on her forehead which was the remains of an accident which she had met with while playing when she was a little girl, and it sort of made her look quite horrible, especially at nights after the lights were put off.

When his father had brought her proposal for him, he had been quite disappointed.

"I don't like the way she looks. I want a very beautiful wife. After all I have to spend the rest of my life with her and also have children from her. I don't want to spend the rest of my life with a woman I don't find attractive."

His father had but made him understand the reasons a man married for.

"You don't get married to spend your life with a beautiful woman. You get married to a woman who will be a good care taker and who will take charge of your house sensibly. A beautiful wife will only empty your pockets with demands of lipsticks and powders to enhance her beauty. After your mother's death, I have done enough for you two brothers and I feel it is time now that one of you took charge. Your elder brother is a good for nothing fellow. He was never good in his studies too. I don't really expect much from him and in any case, who will give their daughter to such a good for nothing fellow? But I do have hope in you. If you bring home a good wife, I will get to relax in my old age."

And so Santosh had got married to Shanti. In the beginning he had thought that he would, as a matter of habit, begin to love her with the passing of the days, but it hadn't been so. He had never been able to fall in love with this woman, though she had in time born him two children. Even without love she had served the purpose of that time. It was some fear due to which in spite of an unwillingness to get tied down, he had tied the knot not really knowing then, that his partner would leave a loose loop to untie it soon after.

It was when Anila and Ankit were only five and two and a half, that Shanti had just left home all of a sudden without giving him the slightest hint of unhappiness. It was late at night when he had returned home from the police station and gone to put his vexed head on the pillow that his eyes had caught sight of a folded piece of paper. He couldn't till date believe what he had then read. She had left a letter for him where she had expressed her point of view, telling him how uneasy she had been in his house, which she had with everyday efforts tried to transform into a home.

"Life with you has been an insult to my womanhood. I have always known that the scar on my forehead is the reason for scaring my life. When as a little girl I had fallen and hurt myself I hadn't realised that the mark my fall had left on me would shed pain throughout my life. I hadn't then known, that outward beauty could be so important; but you have painfully made me realise that every day since I have come to your house. I wish my parents hadn't forced me to get married to you. They too perhaps were worried about who would get married to me and the moment your proposal arrived, they latched me on to you without my consent. If I had my consent, I would have never accepted your proposal. I had always wanted a man of superior intelligence who dwelled in thoughts beyond the body to scale heights of the soul within and I had rightly guessed after meeting you that you weren't of that kind. But I wasn't that lucky to express my choice. The place I came from, women didn't have any choices. I accepted my fate and moved into your house hoping for the best. But it was not to be. Perhaps it is late now to seek freedom but yet I can't but help desire it and move towards it. Do not please make a farce to search for me as you really have never wanted me. The world I know will blame me for being a bad mother, for how could ever, a good mother leave her children behind? But then the world will also never understand the beatings of the heart of a mother who can never give up on her womanly self, even after being a mother."

He had put back the paper after folding it. It was unbelievable. He just couldn't understand how a woman, who had a husband by her side, children to take care of and a house to live in, could yet continue to be unhappy. Life, as he had seen it, was so tightly packed with duties, to have any free time to allow unhappiness to filter in through the window of the routine time-table. He had always been a workaholic himself and thought such people to be funny who searched for happy moments beyond their regular chores.

"Nonsense! I always knew that the woman was crazy." He didn't actually feel forsaken but instead free from the irrational demands of the soul and stuff like that. But as the days passed by, Shanti's absence began to play its role. The house gradually began to look dirtier; the unwashed clothes had piled up in the corner of the room. Things had begun to go missing or couldn't be found in their right places. The children were too small to take charge and the old father and the elder brother had by now due to a woman's presence in the house, got used to taking things for granted.

Life had become hell for him. He had sort of become like a star in the film of his life where he incessantly played a double role. Within the four walls he played the part of a woman, doing all the household chores and outside the house he continued playing the role of being a bread earner.

It was then, after days and nights of tiresome labour that he had decided to get married again. After all, sweeping, swabbing, washing of clothes and utensils was not a man's job. This time however it was just a court marriage sans any guests and gifts or priests and prayers. This time it was just the signing of papers of agreement to be man and wife.

****

Today, as Santosh slung the work bag round his shoulder before leaving for work, he took a quick look at himself in the mirror and noticed a glow on his otherwise recent dull face. The same was quick to be noticed even by his colleagues.

"Wow Santosh, God certainly is partial. He didn't take much time to shower another wife on you. You really are a lucky man".

Santosh smiled and said, "Yes my friend, I really am so relived. I feel so free now. She does all the sweeping, swabbing and cooking to my relief."

THE SHORT SKIRT

Rashmi was a beautiful girl. It was only a few days back that she had celebrated her eighteenth birthday in the usual small way her middle class family was accustomed to. Her mother had made a simple sweet dish with milk, vermicelli and sugar; she had worn new clothes and the family had gone to a temple to seek blessings and thank God for the good health of her body temple.

At last she was an adult. Rashmi had waited for this day endlessly. Becoming an adult was a very prestigious and liberating experience as adults could do whatever they wanted. They could do what they wanted without the compulsions of consulting their elders and after all, there was a certain air of importance given to adults everywhere.

It was a beautiful Sunday morning and to add to her pleasure, her dad was at home. Since he had to go out for some work, he offered his darling daughter to make the best of the opportunity for practicing her driving lesson with him. Yes, one of the great reasons why Rashmi had wanted to become eighteen was to begin to drive. All youngsters had this passion to be behind the wheel and she was no different. She had already made big plans about where all she would drive to with her friends once she had got the license to drive.

Her dad appeared to be in a hurry and so without wasting any time she hurriedly got ready to accompany him by quickly getting into a smart pink top and a black short skirt.

"Let's move on dad, I'm ready." Her dad though appeared not too pleased with the clothes she was wearing and his face showed his dislike immediately.

"What is this you are wearing? Go change into something decent. And hurry up; I don't have time to waste." Her father was a man of few words and everybody at home, including her mother and her two younger brothers always paid attention with immense respect to whatever little he spoke.

Unable to understand why the head of the family was not pleased with her clothes and dressing style, she obviously got upset. "Dad, what's wrong with what I am wearing?" she asked innocently but there was anger in her tone.

Her father's eyes looked too big now to stay comfortable in their sockets. He turned angrily to her mother and then again at her and spoke roughly. "The skirt is too short. Wear something longer, and hurry up if you are seriously interested in coming along for the drive."

The length of a girl's skirt mattered in India. The longer her skirt, the more virtuous she was claimed to be. Her respect as if lay not in her character, but in the clothes with which she covered her body. If the length of her clothes got shorter, negative adjectives attributed to the fall from a feminine glory of the goddess like position was soon without any hesitation attributed to her. Women in India were ironically raised to pedestals of heavenly abode with their status in the temples like that of Laxmi the goddess of wealth, or Saraswati the goddess of wisdom, or Kali the goddess of power of righteousness over evil; but behind the temple walls one heard of different stories of Dev Daasis, who were kept reserved in the name of service to the priests who worshipped those goddesses and for the entertainment of their piously deceptive self which outwardly enacted the performance of a dutiful spirit of reverence and devotion; but once the temple doors were shut, their overmastering desires and passions were let out to the sorrow of those very women in the temple service.

It was sheer mockery of the worthiness of a value system where, in such a hypocritical environment a woman who showed her legs was often considered a slut.

'Look at those legs. She wants it. Why would she otherwise display them in public?' is what the land consisting of many pious men and women spoke.

Rashmi wanted to scream out her independence. She was now eighteen and like any other eighteen year old, she also loved to wear fancy modern clothes. To top it all, she also had a body to carry them off. But she didn't want a tamasha at home and of course if she had continued to prove her point of view and argued, then it would just have led to a battle of words and in fact she would have lost the opportunity to practice at the wheel in the rage which would have followed.

However, with all the politeness and tact of the convincing skills she had learnt by observing her mother for years, she made an attempt to get her point across to her father. "It's not that short daddy. And any way I'm just going to be seated in the car with you." But the senior refused to be convinced and spoke even more with hurried anger. "Either you change or you stay back home."

Now Rashmi was helpless. If she argued her dad's order any further, she would certainly miss out on the driving. Being a smart girl, she chose to therefore make use of situational wisdom and humbly lost the battle of free choice.

"You know too well how important a driving class is to me and you're hardly at home on week days to take me out."

"Well then make up your mind. I was to take you out, but if you prefer your short skirt, then you'd rather sit at home in it."

"That's not fair. Everybody wears such skirts. They are the 'in thing'.

She turned to her mother for emotional help.

"Can't you say something to him? Why don't you make him understand? It's my life and I'm an adult now. I must be allowed to do what I want to and wear what I think suits me and especially so if I'm comfortable in it.

Her mother was of no help.

"My darling child, it's our society that chains us, not allowing us to use our freedom. We Indians believe in covering our bodies. It's a different mind-set over here. If you were in some foreign land where clothes or rather lack of them weren't given so much importance, then perhaps your father wouldn't have objected as he does now. He's just a normal Indian father. He wants to protect you because he loves you."

"But nothing is happening to me. And why would anything in the world happen to me by wearing a short skirt? What exactly is he trying to protect me from? Daddy is wearing shorts himself. Why doesn't the Indian society have a problem with men who show their legs? Why these double standards?"

The father was getting too impatient by now. "This is my last call to you Rashmi. Are you coming for a drive or shall I move out alone? I have some work to catch up with. I thought that you could have driven me there and got the practice you needed."

By now Rashmi had given up. "Wait a minute daddy. It takes a young girl time to change her clothes. And I need something that is going to match with this top now."

She quickly went to her room to search through her cupboard and hurriedly changed into a long skirt which had a lovely floral print on it.

Back besides her father within a few moments, she expressed her dislike towards the parental authority he had imposed on her "Will this do now? Do I look more respectable now? Am I now dressed appropriately to drive you to your work?" her dad did not respond. "Dad is this okay?" she swirled around her father holding the edges of the long skirt in both hands as if she were giving a dance performance.

Her father laughed and hugged his darling daughter. They moved out on to the street where the car was parked.

****

"You drive quite well you know? Only a few more lessons and I think you'll be done. Don't forget to look into the rear mirror before you change the lane."

But to Rashmi's horror, what did she see? There was a stark naked man walking in the middle of the road. As her father saw him too, he slammed his thigh in disgust. "Oh!

Damn it. These bikshus must be banned on the streets. They should follow their religion behind closed doors in all their nakedness." There was a young man totally naked on the street. He was no mad man or a beggar but a man who belonged to a religious sect in India, which believed that it was nature that clothed them and therefore there arouse no necessity of any material for the covering of their bodies.

Rashmi looked at her father and smiled. "See dad, no harm has ever come to these naked men. You were worried for no reason about my short skirt."

TROUBLE

This was not an everyday sight. To watch a woman bathing in the open was not a sight one's eyes perceived every day; in fact it was abnormal. Not that his eyes didn't want that cooling experience, but no woman who had the slightest decency would choose to lay bare her body for a lustful vision while bathing in the open.

Her skin appeared as if it was soaking in all the water falling on it to quench its thirst for cleansing. With only a white cotton dupatta, once curling round her hips and the rest flung across her right shoulder, the curves of her anatomy were erotic indeed. She had moved out of all the enclosures of decency as if she required none whatsoever.

The book of her life had pages in it which had been splattered with colours of incest within the four walls of her own house. She longed to get them washed away. The water falling on her body was as if effectively cleansing off her emotions appealing for some relief. There was too much impurity her eyes had seen and now it seemed as if only the rains could remove the defilement away. The Gods looking down from the heavens above were helping her to scrub out the pain in her heart through her eyes, as no one could tell the difference between water from the above and water from the recesses of her heart dripping down secretly onto her cheeks.

Every gesture of hers looked artistically graceful to him, as if there was some aesthetic performance taking place; he silently kept watching. He wished he could have gone ahead and introduced himself and touched that brown flesh underneath the white cloth which unsuccessfully and partially covered it. It was too early in the morning for anybody to have woken up and crossed their threshold to begin their daily chores. Deep down, he was grateful to himself for his regular habit of waking up early in the mornings. Be it a working day or a holiday, he was an early riser, and that today had certainly done him good. He wondered if she disrobed, exposing herself like that every day and cursed himself for missing a sight so astonishingly and sensationally magnificent before.

Actually, he hadn't much noticed her earlier except for a few times when he had waited at the grocery shop outside their building to light a match for a quick smoke and she had hurriedly passed by holding the hand of a little pig tailed girl. Who would have ever thought then, that under those bulky cotton saris were hidden some great and desirable proportions.

As he was engrossed watching her, his heart skipped a beat and he wished that he had found her earlier than her husband had.

It had stopped raining and yet she continued to be there moving her hands on her body as if she were scrubbing herself, rubbing off something on it which was not wanting to detach itself from her skin. As she moved, the white cloth kept slipping away to expose more of her already exposed skin and then suddenly to his dismay, she gathered herself and went away indoors.

Then, during the rest of the day as he went about doing his work, he realized that she had stayed on with him. In fact, her almost naked vision had got glued on to his eyes. A few days later, when one evening he was returning home from work in his car, he saw her rushing with difficulty as she seemed to be limping. Not wanting to miss out on the opportunity to get to know her better, he called out.

"Hi, I'm Gulshan, may I be of some help? I just stay across the street." Quite without being courteous and without any words, she helped herself into his car.

Sitting herself in the seat next to his she said, "I'm so grateful, really I'm so thankful to you. You really are God sent." It seemed quite exaggerated and verbosely ridiculous to him, as after all the distance from where she sat in his car to her house was just some ten minutes and she could have easily limped till there in double the time. In fact a lady of honour would have probably refused the lift.

She continued, "These roads are getting worse day by day, especially in the rains. To my bad luck, my sandal strap broke and I'm in such a rush that I have no time to wait to get it stitched. I really have to thank you a lot."

He wondered at what the hurry could have been for and politely asked, "Is there an emergency at home? Your face is a picture of worry."

She suddenly fell silent.

"My daughter is waiting for me. She is alone."

"Oh! Don't worry, when I was leaving an hour ago I saw your husband returning. You can be relaxed now; your daughter will be having her father by her side."

His words to his surprise lit a match to a gas spill. "What are you saying? Oh my God!"

The car had reached her house by then and she flung opened the door of the vehicle and rushed out with the sandals in her hand without even turning once to say a polite thank-you.

Though it had been a limited conversation of not more than a few minutes, the momentous togetherness had left him totally confused. Some basic instinct told him that there had to be a problem which was refraining from speech, and yet screaming for help. She was either in deep trouble or completely mad to behave the way she just had. After all, which respectable woman living in a middle class residential area came out in just her skin and a transparent drape to enjoy a downpour? He wanted to help; but how could he barge into her private world and save her? What could he possibly do, just go at her door and say, 'You have a problem lady? May I help?' It would all seem so ridiculous.

That night sleep refused to come to his comfort; and to give a topping to the cerebral anguish which kept him awake, it kept drizzling outside. The sound of the softness of the rain drops on his window pane set him into a rhythm of thought. A countless times he relived the journey of the lift incident in his mind's recording system where he played and paused and pressed the rewind button a plentiful of times.

He remembered distinctly how she had exclaimed, "Oh my God!" It had seemed too odd for his ears to adjust normally to that exclamation from a woman who had been told about her husband being at home. Of course he had understood the undercurrents hidden behind that exclamation. There had to be some discontent in her life.

The confusion however was as to where could he locate it. He was somewhat sure that trouble lay within the four walls of her house. He remembered seeing her quite often with her daughter but never with her husband.

Probably they didn't get along; probably he often lost his temper on the child; or he could be the violent kind who didn't hesitate in lifting his hand on the slightest pretext to beat the kid. It could be any of these reasons why she had appeared so edgy. But if he remembered well, he had seen the man a few times and he hadn't appeared the violent kind at all. In fact he had seemed to look quite docile but then looks could be deceptive. He had hardly seen him talk to anyone. In fact he seemed quite a passive fellow to cause much trouble. But again who knew, silent waters did run deep. In his school days he had read a lot of Hitchcock and was always fascinated by the investigations of the detective. Now a thrill was knocking at his door and he had to exercise his brain but who would be his Dr. Watson? He would have to make smart moves. The case would never reach its conclusion from his balcony.

The next thing he knew, he was keeping tabs on her house. He didn't mind changing the look of his home décor but he had to do it all, if he wanted to search for a solution to the mystery. Shifting his work desk closer to the window gave him a better picture of his work field. He began maintaining records of every entry and exit, every pace of walk and every expression on the faces that he could see moving about in that house.

After about two weeks of a thorough detective kind of observation, he came to the conclusion that the issue had to be a sensitive one. The husband always seemed to have had a satisfied look on his face and yet her face appeared a picture of worry and weariness.

Probably it would be better, he thought to himself to close the case as there was nothing much in it; or probably he had failed as a detective. And in any case, he knew that he would never be able to trespass the four walls of that house and the glass in her eyes. Unless she decided to come out in the open and shed a few tears, he could not hold up a handkerchief and help her to wipe them off. Of course there was some trouble lurking over there, but trouble was there in many other places in the world; waiting to be rescued to a trouble free zone. It never happened though. Trouble needed to take a bold step forward and ask for help; and he knew that most troubles were scared to peep out from under the heavy coverings of blankets of fear to take a look out into the bright sunlight of freedom.

It made no sense wasting his time waiting for that gutless trouble to own up to its problems and step out in the open. He had a life of his own and he had to move on.

WET PANTIES

As she sat at the wheel, she felt an urgent need to loosen the seat belt on her waist. If only she had known that she would have been getting stuck up at the signal for such an atrociously long time, she would have refrained from having a second cup of tea before leaving home. Now all that favourite liquid of hers was causing havoc on her bladder. The normal thirty minutes' drive to work had already taken more than two hours.

She remembered how almost a decade back she had laid on the birthing bed in the hospital, surrounded with all the assisting staff urging her to urinate after she had with all the force within her and with great efforts managed to push out the twins; and then due to all the exertion had collapsed physically and emotionally.

"Push, push, you are doing well; a little more, it's important, don't give up." She could keep hearing those words which were breaking into her bliss after the long stretch of exhaustion.

"It's not happening. What do I do?"

"It's important. Try as much as you can or else, we will have to put a catheter."

Probably they had just been scaring her. She wondered why urinating could be so damn important? They had told that if the bladder were to get too full then she wouldn't be able to pass urine and then the catheter would be inserted which would probably cause problems of its own. She had grown up to believe that it was quite a nuisance necessity in her country for most women who had no decent place to go and relieve themselves unlike the men, who unzipped themselves in moments of pressure under any tree or any nook and corner of the streets. God alone knew why her bladder then had refused to pay heed to the warnings of those attendants surrounding her. It had probably got influenced by her stubborn nature. The word 'catheter' had though managed to scare the wits out of her new found moment of joy; after all not all women gave birth to twins. A few moments ago she was enjoying the warmth of her new motherhood and the next moment she was being warned about the repercussions if she didn't obey. She had heard stories of pain and infections which followed the procedure of the catheter, and in fact she had just completed a marathon time of the most painful experience a woman could go through. Perhaps that fear was then responsible for the water that had trickled out soon to everybody's relief. "It's done; it's done." The attendant had shouted out with a relieved voice.

"Now you may go to sleep."

Ah! What a sigh of relief she had taken. Finally they had left her all by herself to enjoy the bliss of her maternal rapture.

****

Today however it was something really crazy happening on the streets of Mumbai. Some school was having a fight with its management authorities. The management wanted to shift the students to another place and open up an international school at the present premises. Obviously the parents didn't want that, for if they wished their children to continue their studies at the international level it would burden their shoulders with a rise in the fee structure and if they agreed to shift to another place, the distance from their homes to the school would be problem for the child as well as the parents as the commuting time would surely change. As a last shot of an attempt to survive and fight for the old pattern of education to continue, they had brought out their kids on the streets; and those little ones were made to take a long nap on the concrete flooring of the road under the hot sun, disrupting the entire city's speed of work. It was like washing ones dirty linen in public, but probably they had been nudged too deep to have taken such a hell raising step. Sometimes, she felt it became necessary for the eradication of certain evils to bring them out unconcealed for the masses to recognize and let the filth and smell of their stench get publicly known.

She was by now caught in the traffic at the Hajji Ali Junction for more than two hours and her bladder was asking for an urgent release. The Hajji Ali was a tourist spot and in fact considered as one of the seven wonders in the world, with a mosque built in the middle of the Arabian Sea which thousands of Muslims and non-Muslims visited daily, either for prayers or just to marvel at the construction. How she wished at the time that her bladder would like those many years back get stubborn once again and save her the embarrassment on the road; but it had instead as if become her enemy. She tried taking deep breaths to ease her scared mind. What if her bladder broke the dam of control? Her place of work was yet far away and there was no way to turn back and go home. The cars stood bumper to bumper. There were beautiful songs playing on the radio, in fact some of them were her all-time favourites but her anxiety of probable embarrassment was not allowing her to enjoy the music. She also unclasped the seat belt, not wanting any external pressure on the already escalating pressure from within. It was as if she was stuck in the middle of a sea of cars. She could see men get out from their cars around her and step onto the foot-paths to unzip themselves under trees there.

Oh God! How she wished she were a man. Men were shrewd, smart, calculating, opportunists and best of all they were environmentalists. They helped the growth of foliage all around the city. They felt no shame! For once she almost hated herself for being a woman. It was getting unbearable for her. She had to be strong and shameless. But how could she? God! For once she had to stop thinking of what the others would think of her. But how could she? She had to just get out and relieve herself. But how could she? She almost felt like opening the front and rear doors and telling the guy sitting in the car to her right to turn his face to the other side and then quickly sit in between the two doors and not be bothered about the guy behind her car seeing water trickle down the road. But her legs remained stiff refusing to budge, as if they had gone numb. She was sort of angry with them for not having any guts to do what her mind wanted them to. She wished that the government instead of concentrating on the big multiplexes and malls would instead for the women of the country focus its attention to public toilets. Yes great revolutions had taken place for women in this land; abolishment of sati, widow remarriage, free education for the girl child and the various benefits that the girl child parents got, were indeed applaudable. The government had put in a lot of its energy to educate the masses about the value of a woman by advertising vigorously against female infanticide but it had completely overlooked the basic need of a woman to urinate.

Her memory took her to her college days when she used to learn the French language and visit the Alliance Francis class near the Taj Mahal Hotel at Colaba. The class was well equipped with audio aids and air conditioning but it had over looked the need of a wash room. She had been angry then at such disregard. She remembered the letter she had written to a daily newspaper venting out her anger at the failure of the need of attention to be focused on full bladders of women. 'Pis-Aller', her letter in the newspaper 'The Daily', hadn't made any difference even after so many years. In fact now she had been told that the class had changed its location and even if it hadn't, she thought, after Kasab's visit to the five star hotels, the security there wouldn't even allow the use of their wash rooms any more to outsiders.

To her relief, suddenly the traffic seemed to have eased and she quickly began changing gears as her eyes desperately searched for a public toilet. What a sigh escaped her mouth when she saw one on the crowded road near The Bhatia Hospital. There was no time to think now. She just moved the car to the side of the road, stopped, locked the vehicle and was into the semi stinking place. How every minute she was praising God for the great escape He had offered her.

Probably not many women in the villages and various cities of her land had gone through similar escapes from humiliation. She smiled at the jubilation of such an escape and wondered how a country where women were raised up to reach the sky and touch the horizons had failed to pay attention to the basic need of the female sex leaving her to feel embarrassed with wet panties.

WITHOUT EYES

She had often heard people say that eyes were windows to one's soul. A thought that bothered Pranali often, was how she would manage to successfully look into her daughter's soul? When a child was born it had no language but that of the one spoken with the help of the eyes. Happiness could be seen in the sparkle of the vision and sadness melted out in tears.

Kinjal was a beautiful and bubbly child but at the age of three she had succumbed to some infection in her eyes. The family doctor's advice was taken into consideration and eye drops were put into her eyes, to her discomfort. However something somewhere certainly had gone wrong and the child had gradually lost her sight.

Pranali had been heartbroken. Her family and friends had tried to console her in her grief but there had been no end to her suffering. Kinjal was her life and it had been heart breaking to see her life turn dark. Some people around her had vociferated that it was the doing of the Gods and some had said that perhaps it was some ancestral curse. Her educated mind had felt that if the Gods were to be held responsible then they were not worthy of their Godhood and in any case her mind had always been groomed with the knowledge of science which strongly prohibited her from believing that blindness could ever get transferred from one generation to another and certainly not at least through the pathway of curses.

Her mother then grey, with wisdom accumulated with age, had felt that it certainly would do no harm to appease the furious Gods by performing some special prayers which could get back the eyesight of her grand-daughter.

"Pranali, I understand and respect your modern scientific thoughts; but what harm would it do to you by going and asking for forgiveness at reverential sites? Certainly you as a mother wouldn't mind doing that for your child."

But Pranali was adamant. She just couldn't understand what act of her behaviour had caused the suffering to her child and how the child could be now saved from its grip by her seeking forgiveness.

"Ma, blindness is not transferred from one generation to the other. Yes, what gets transferred is a set of blind beliefs; beliefs that have no factual base but instead rest on a firm ground of prejudice to get a grip on the rough road of survival."

Pranali could never forget the day when her neighbour, Aunty Molly had come over to meet her mother and expressed some superstition of hers to the emotionally susceptible woman.

"Urvashi, believe me or not but that bitter Neem tree in your garden which you Hindu people revere, is the cause of bitterness in your daughter and grand-daughter's life. I have often seen Kinjal sitting under its shade and playing for hours on end. That tree I believe has shed its bitterness into your child's life. In our Holy Bible, we are instructed to not revere anything other than the Lord our God and if we disobey the Lord, He surely gets angry on us. I know you will find me foolish, but please pray to Jesus and ask for His forgiveness for your errors and He will surely restore your grand-daughter's eyesight."

When Pranali heard what Aunt Molly had conveyed to her mother, she got furious at her mother for entertaining such baseless beliefs. The old lady if she were not a friend of her mother's would have got a piece of her mind. "Mother, what rubbish is that woman talking! The Neem tree shedding its bitterness into our lives! How atrocious can people get? Why didn't you make her understand that we revere that tree because of its antiseptic qualities and that we chew on its bitter leaves to do away with killer diseases like diabetes? That woman I think loves to wear and flaunt her dark glasses of ignorance and neglect the bright sunlight of knowledge."

Time had moved on doing its work and Kinjal had grown up into a beautiful woman oblivious of her gorgeous looks. Her mother's constant support had helped her to move on smilingly. She had to accept that though it had not been a bed of roses for her, her mother's strength had protected her from wearing a blanket of thorns.

Perhaps it was the positive outlook of her mother, which had filled every moment in her life with brightness and her father's calm that had helped her withstand the storms of life which at times drowned even those with eyesight. Her parents had been a great support and encouragement and were responsible for the sunny smile on her face even though some one up there behind the clouds had drawn dark curtains over her eyes. Time had done a good job by pulling on her limbs to make her attractively tall and her mind to make her intellectual vision broader.

Call it luck or her intelligence; she had managed to meet Yuvraj who had turned out to be a lovely life partner. Her marriage had helped her parents smile a smile of confidence after all the years of her growing up; after all every parent wanted their child to get settled in life. Yuvraj was a handsome man who she had met at her college. Her beauty and confidence in spite of her handicap had attracted the young man to her and a friendship had blossomed to grow into a beautiful relationship culminating into the tying of the knot.

Many a physically attractive and able bodied girls would have matched Yuvraj better, but he had chosen her nature and mind over their beauty and in spite of her handicap had proposed marriage to her. Their union had brought into their lives a beautiful healthy male child whom they named Vishal. Vishal, which meant greatness; exemplified the greatness of man's mind to search deep into the soul of the other tearing through the veils of superficial bodily beauty and have a union with the person hidden deep inside the cage of the body. This child as he grew up became a great binding glue in his parent's book of life which had the text of true love written in it. However, he was the only child they had dared to bring into the world because it was not easy for her to take care of so demanding an individual.

****

kinjal now was an old woman. She had passed her life with the help of great souls like her grand-mother, a very strong mother, a calm father and a very loving husband. When she had lost her eyesight, she had been too young to remember the faces of her parents or her grand-mother but her soul had seen the beauty of their hearts which had filled her dark world with opportunities of making it into a colourful canvas.

As she combed her hair, she wondered how many black strands she had left in the memory of her youth. As a child she had seen her grandmother's grey head which had been etched in her mind's eye and she very well remembered how it looked, though the old woman's face had got lost in the span of life. She wondered whom she looked like; whether she resembled her grandmother or her mother. But how did it matter now?

She spent her days sitting alone wondering about the looks of her son, the second man in her life. She often also wondered about the kind of features her daughter-in-law had. Yuvraj had moved on with his life, leaving her companionless in her dark world. His passing away had hurt her and it had been a hurt which had surpassed all the other hurts of her life. Even her turning blind had not been that painful as her husband's death. She had sobbed and sobbed that day almost being inconsolable as now the one through whom she had seen love had shut his eyes forever.

If she had been able to play with the curls on her son's head, it had been with her fingers but through Yuvraj's eyes. Though she had changed her son's nappies with the love and wisdom of motherhood, she had revelled in being a mother through Yuvraj who had described her child to her. Yuvraj had been determined to make it good with her and their life together had proved that even the differently abled could live happily ever after with the normally abled.

He had lead her into a beautiful married life encouraging her in spite of her many faltering steps to believe that physical disability was not enough reason to deter from leading a normal happy life. If 'happiness was a state of mind', then he had filled her mind with happy short moments of joy which her long life even without him could today reflect on with tears of joy.

Today, she often sat alone with her eyes looking inwards at the kaleidoscope of memories as her son and daughter in-law went around doing their daily chores. She wondered if one had to have a constant replenishment of activities to be happy. As she sat with her remembrances, she felt happy that they occupied her in retrospection.

READING TO TOMMY

Children in India were always excited at the mention of summer holidays, but for Kishori this time of the year was a time to be dreaded. It was that time of the year which stressed her out unlike some other children who looked forward to this amazing period of lazing around and relaxing after a year full of activities, assignments and examinations at school. At times she wished that the school would just give them a maximal of a day or twos break and start over with the new academic year without that long vacation period. She loved her parents; she loved her grandparents even more and most of all she loved to stay at home, playing with her little brother who had just learnt to walk his first few tiny steps. She was worried though, that when he too grew up, her parents would begin to trouble him as they did her with all their magnified ideas of their expertise in recognising hidden abilities to locate concealed talents; packing him off like they did her to the various activity classes.

The recess bell had rung but she had been so lost in thoughts that she had missed hearing it. All the kids around her had begun their shuffling and pushing to get out into the corridors of freedom from the classroom constrictions, but Kishori continued to sit glued to the bench lost in thoughts.

Ms. D'Mello loved this sweet little quite child. She called out to her from her table.

'Kishori aren't you going out for the short break?'

But the child seemed to be lost in some contemplation and gave no answer.

"Kishori", this time the teacher's voice was quite loud to miss the girl's ears. "Please come here". Kishori quickly got up straightening her uniform and moved agilely in the cramped space between the desks to Ms. D'Mello.

'Yes teacher?'

'Kishori, it is break time. Why aren't you joining your friends with your tiffin box?'

'Sorry teacher I'll get my tiffin and go'.

The child moved back towards her school bag to get the packed sandwiches her mum usually gave her to take to school. She didn't really mind eating them as a snack; but what she would have preferred were burgers and pizzas and pastries but that was never to be as her mum would lecture her on the nutritive value of the sandwiches and she had learnt to keep her mouth shut because in any case she was never allowed to indulge in what gave her simple fun without some purpose attached to it. Walking back towards the corridor she opened her tiffin box and picked up the brown bread stuffed with crunchy vegetables in it. Just when she was about to put the meal to her mouth, she suddenly remembered her mother adding a cookery class to her holiday's agenda. That terrible thought suddenly as if killed her appetite and she put the bread back in the box and with a put-on smile offered its contents to the girls around her. Many hands instantly made their way into the tiffin and in a few minutes Kishori shut the lid on its empty clean self.

Kishori didn't mind eating tasty and nutritious sandwiches but she simply wanted to eat them. She was not interested in going to Bharati anunty's class with another eight to ten kids; standing around the kitchen table in her house and see the demonstration of their making. She wanted to sit in a comfortable rocking chair in front of the television and munch into some tasty stuff as she rocked herself to the joy of eating as well as excitingly watching those funny cartoons. She was not allowed to view cartoons though. Her television viewing was timed and restricted to the History Channel and the Discovery Channel. She had to compulsorily watch the great discoveries of the world at the cost of losing her childhood, and she hated to hear 'His-story' as she wanted to live her own. She wanted to cry out loud and scream but cautioned herself, for if she did that, probably her father, a self-claimed genius, would locate some talent in her voice and arrange for a voice modulation class making a total ass of her. She was not a dumb child and yet she couldn't understand her parents. They said they loved her; well if they did, she thought, why did they rob her off all the fun in her life?

Her father, like a chorus in a song had a few lines which he kept repeating to her, 'Kishori you are a very clever girl. You are going to become someone great one day'. But she didn't want to become great. She wanted to remain small and happy and just play and have fun. She wanted to be average. Was that bad? She wondered if it was not alright to be average. The vacation classes during the last holidays she remembered had got her sick to the core. Her holidays used to begin at five in the morning with a tennis class, followed by six laps of swimming at the pool, and then a run to the pool canteen to grab a few bites of an egg omelette as she needed a high protein diet with all the energy she was using up. The breakfast was followed by an hours rest period which she had to take in the car as her dad's driver drove her to Ms. Mathai's elocution class. Of late she had begun to stutter and Ms. Mathai had brought this newly acquired defect in her speech to her parent's attention. To her grief though, no body at home understood why words were failing to escape fluently from her lips. Instead, both her parents took turns to make her practice more speech before retiring to bed every night. 'Why are you being miserly with your words?' her mother screamed at her.

'What is this I, I, I, I, I, I? Just let that I out of your mouth. Don't hold on to it and move on to the other words.'

She wanted to scream out, 'I want to be left alone. I want to play. I want to waste my time. I want to sleep till late; these are my holidays Mum! I want to be free to do what I want and not what you want me to do'.

But she held back her scream because she knew that her mother would give her deaf ears and probably even if she did hear her, she would not be concentrating on what she was saying but instead she would be all ears on the pitch and the sound and the pronunciation of every word she uttered. So she kept her mouth shut and her tears remained packed tight in her dreamy eyes half shut as she kept her head bent, focusing at her feet.

'Okay Kishori', her mother got up to finally leave her alone. 'I think you'd better go to sleep. Tomorrow is Sunday and you know we have to be at the Crossword Bookstore'. Yes of course she knew! How could she forget her every Sunday being spoilt by sitting in the midst of a heaven of fantasies but being allowed to read only about facts? She had to read about the first woman pilot, the first man to land on moon, the first plane to have spread its wings like a bird, the First World War and the list never seemed to end.

The next morning, dressed in a beautiful floral pink dress, which in spite of its bright colourful splash failed to bring a vibrant shade to her grey feelings, she walked into the famous bookstore of the city. To her surprise though, the scene there was unnerving. There was a big brown dog sitting on a carpet specially spread out for him in the middle of the children's corner and there were so many children sitting all around him. Her eyes suddenly sparkled with joy at the sight of the furry animal.

'Uncle', she asked an attendant standing nearby, 'May I touch him?'

'Yes of course you may. He's all yours. Come let me introduce you to him'.

The young attendant took hold of her hand and led her to the canine. Skilfully, he managed to make some place for her to sit comfortably close to the animal and spoke in his ear, 'Hi Tommy! We have a little friend here for you. She's going to read to you'. Looking at Kishori he said, 'Tell him your name. Introduce yourself and here, take this book of fairy tales and read to him. He's a good listener and he loves stories. Will you read to him?' Kishori's cheeks seemed to have suddenly acquired a colour to them and her dimples cut in deep.

'Yes uncle, I would love to.' She took the book from his hands and began reading.

'Once upon a time there was a little girl. One day, as she was going home from school, she saw a hill-lock. Oh! She

wondered how she had missed seeing it earlier. She walked close to it and felt like climbing its small height. She knew that her mother would be upset with her as she would be wasting a lot of study time, but then she wanted to waste her time and so she began to climb. As she climbed the hill she saw beautiful, colourful flowers growing at her feet. They smiled at her as her toes touched their soft petals. She bent down to feel their smoothness and even plucked a few of them and put them in her hair. She climbed higher and higher till she reached the very top. The sun was so close to her now. She could have if she wanted, touched it and burnt her fingers. But she didn't do that because she was a clever girl. She turned to climb down again. The climb had helped her fetch the warmth of the fiery ball with her. She felt good with the energy she had received from the climb. Her steps had by now gathered a bounce in them. They had acquired a speed different from the earlier times. Each step of hers became a hop and then a jump and then she went running home. She was so happy. She put her school bag in its place, gulped down the glass of milk her mother had kept ready for her, washed her hands, changed into her house clothes and opened the school books. Every word there she could understand better now. Oh! She realised that it was the magic of the sunshine.'

No sooner had she finished reading, her ears suddenly heard a loud clapping. She felt embarrassed. She was a heroine this morning. She had read the story without a stutter because Tommy had been listening to her and she knew that he would never criticise her or ridicule her or correct her. It was the most lovely holiday time she had had in many days.